Stories by Contemporary Writers from Shanghai

SHE SHE

This book is edited and designed by the Editorial Committee of *Cultural China* series

Text by Zou Zou
Translation by Yawtsong Lee
Cover Image by Getty Images
Interior Design by Xue Wenqing
Cover Design by Wang Wei

Copy Editor: Susan Luu Xiang
Editor: Wu Yuezhou
Editor-in-chief: Zhang Yicong

Senior Consultants: Sun Yong, Wu Ying, Yang Xinci
Managing Director and Publisher: Wang Youbu

ISBN: 978-1-60220-239-9

Address any comments about *She She* to:

Better Link Press
99 Park Ave
New York, NY 10016
USA

or

Shanghai Press and Publishing Development Company
F 7 Donghu Road, Shanghai, China (200031)
Email: comments_betterlinkpress@hotmail.com

Printed in China by Shanghai Donnelley Printing Co., Ltd.

1 3 5 7 9 10 8 6 4 2

SHE SHE

By Zou Zou

Better Link Press

Foreword

This collection of books for English readers consists of short stories and novellas published by writers based in Shanghai. Apart from a few who are immigrants to Shanghai, most of them were born in the city, from the latter part of the 1940s to the 1980s. Some of them had their works published in the late 1970s and the early 1980s; some gained recognition only in the 21st century. The older among them were the focus of the "To the Mountains and Villages" campaign in their youth, and as a result, lived and worked in the villages. The difficult paths of their lives had given them unique experiences and perspectives prior to their eventual return to Shanghai. They took up creative writing for different reasons but all share a creative urge and a love for writing. By profession, some of them are college professors, some literary editors, some directors of literary institutions, some freelance writers and some professional writers. From the individual styles of the authors and the art of their writings, readers can easily detect traces of the authors' own experiences in life, their interests, as well as their aesthetic values. Most of the works in this collection are still written in the realistic style that represents, in a painstakingly fashioned fictional world, the changes of the times in urban and rural life. Having grown up in a more open era, the younger writers have been spared the hardships experienced by their predecessors, and therefore seek greater freedom in their writing. Whatever category of writers they belong to, all of them have gained their rightful places in the Chinese literary circles over the last forty years. Shanghai writers tend to favor urban narratives more than other genres of writing. Most of the works in this collection can be characterized as urban literature with Shanghai characteristics, but there are also exceptions.

Called the "Paris of the East," Shanghai was already an international metropolis in the 1920s and

30s. Being the center of China's economy, culture and literature at the time, it housed a majority of writers of importance in the history of modern Chinese literature. The list includes Lu Xun, Guo Moruo, Mao Dun and Ba Jin, who had all written and published prolifically in Shanghai. Now, with Shanghai re-emerging as a globalized metropolis, the Shanghai writers who have appeared on the literary scene in the last forty years all face new challenges and literary quests of the times. I am confident that some of the older writers will produce new masterpieces. As for the fledging new generation of writers, we naturally expect them to go far in their long writing careers ahead of them. In due course, we will also introduce those writers who did not make it into this collection.

Wang Jiren

Series Editor

Contents

Abandonment

The day he came home with the baby girl in his arms is still fresh in his mind. He had always desired a son. We're now turning into the little alley that leads to our home. Now we're home. This is the entrance. Now we come up the two steps! This is where we leave our shoes before going upstairs. Here's the dog we keep. We're now on the second floor. This is your room, and this is daddy and mommy's room, but it also belongs to you. He talked to her in a rambling, cheerful, unhurried manner, with a slight querying, upward inflection, as if she could understand what he was saying. And he spoke to her in the normal way, keeping his words as simple as possible without resorting to baby talk and using such words as goo-goo or yum-yum. Now mommy is going to feed you on her breast. You'll drink mommy's milk for about nine months. After that, if milk becomes your favorite food you'll have to settle for cow milk's. We don't know yet which brand of cow's milk is safe. We won't worry about it now. Daddy wishes he could keep a cow just for you. This is Daddy's hand stroking your head. Daddy strokes your head with his left hand because Daddy's a lefty. Mommy's a righty and uses her right hand more. We don't know yet if you'll turn out to be right or left-handed, or better yet, ambidextrous! Now you just lie on Mommy's bosom. Daddy is going out. Here's a kiss for you. Now you're kissing Daddy. You don't know how to kiss yet. Daddy has just pressed your little face to his.

He found it strange that he no longer needed a son, not because she was a baby (which she was), but because, as he was talking to her, he could sense that this was his daughter.

He decided to shed some of his old habits, even giving up the pleasure of reading in bed at night, lest the rustling of the pages might disturb the slumber of his daughter in her crib. He took to sitting for hours at a stretch by her side watching her grow inch by inch. As he saw the baby's fingers ball up and relax and her chest, like his, rise and fall, he imagined she must be dreaming. And what would she be dreaming of? He hadn't dreamed for a long time now. When she woke up crying, he would pick her up and rock her back to sleep in his arms, taking the opportunity to talk to her about things he figured she needed to know. Afterwards he would question the significance of all that to her.

After her, he lost another baby, which had assumed human form but was stillborn. That same year, a friend of his also lost a baby. But she was no longer a baby; by the time she died of illness, she was already two years old. After that tragic event, he would often sit in his study wondering how many young children would be called up to heaven every year.

He felt he was fortunate at least in that he would not lose his wife. No one could take her away from him, except Death. He was her only man, notwithstanding the fact that he often stayed all night in his study. His wife had recently started to dabble in gardening, forever turning up the soil in that little bed. He stayed in his study, encouraging the impression that he was reading or surfing the Web; but the fact was he stood by the window, looking down, through his lenses and the glass pane, at his wife, who had her back turned toward him. At 11:55 p.m. the child's heart stopped, the ER team massaged her heart for half an hour, trying to resuscitate her to no avail. At 12:25 a.m., the doctor pronounced her dead. The days when he and his wife could talk about everything and anything, withholding nothing from each other, were gone for good after the death of their daughter. People carefully stepped around the subject of his daughter, as if her disappearance were nothing out of the ordinary. More than a year later, they began to mention the child again. Maybe they had never noticed that he once had a daughter.

Therefore he was somewhat perplexed one day to find, when he came home after wasting a whole evening roaming the streets, a slip of paper, tucked under the dome-shaped mesh food tent on the dining table. I had to do this for both our sakes.

Why couldn't she have said it to his face? Why didn't she tuck it under a pillow, or put it in some drawer in the wardrobe? They didn't leave notes for each other in their household. When she had something to say, she would text him, such as when supper was ready and she wanted him to come downstairs to the table, or when she wanted him to go to the grocery store with her. A note like this was very unusual in their married life. For both our sakes! How could she make the decision for him?

He made his way upstairs with the note in his

hand. Their room looked no different. Her clothes were gone, but that did not give the impression of a boring, lifeless room. Lying in bed, he repeatedly studied the size A5 sheet of letter paper. It was plain and clean, without any telltale signs of tears rolling off the cheeks of his wife as she wrote hesitantly, pausing at each stroke of the pen.

He was her first man, and her only man. He was convinced of this. Both of them were raised in farming villages, so it was that some things should not have mattered that much, and should have been taken for granted. But he could not rein in his restless imagination. Maybe she was seized by a sudden wanderlust. How much did she have in savings? Was she still contemplating a future that had the two of them together? Or did she crave to leave all this behind and find a more unencumbered place shielded from memories and imposed reality? No, maybe none of this was the true reason. Maybe the truth was she just wanted to free herself of him and go to a place without him.

In the weeks that followed, he could not shake the feeling that his wife was still there, cooking his favorite dishes in the kitchen, standing at the counter with the toe of her right foot resting on the floor, or turning up the soil around the flowers and plants, or calling out to him using his full name. When he finally realized he should feel the pain of his loss, he gently opened the door to his daughter's room and sat down on her bed clutching the note in his hand. I don't know what to do. He left the note on his daughter's bed. Then he tried several places, first under the pillow, where it instantly disappeared from sight. The second time he put it under the bed sheet, but he could still feel it through the fabric. On the third try he rose to his feet and distractedly let the note slip from his hand.

Every few days he would go into his daughter's room, hoping that as he opened the door he would find the note to have vanished, just like his daughter. But it was always there.

During those years he lost his job once. Other things he lost included keys, pens, books, umbrellas, wallets, cell phones, as well as a lot of hair. Previously a burly man, he had also lost some weight. But he did not lose his life, and he did not lose that note, which had stayed in his daughter's room.

Friends tried to interest him in some women. He

would meet with them out of courtesy, but refused to get further acquainted with them. When his friends talked about other women in his presence, or mentioned life's joys, comfort or even happiness, he would smile, amused by the analogy between all these things and the voluminous tomes of *The Man without Qualities* by Robert Musil: they weigh heavily in one's hands, and even though one may not have read them, one can always discuss them and even recommend them to others.

But he did acquire a new habit at the insistence of some friends. Every morning before he left his home he would repeat three times to the person in front of the mirror: I am all right. I am happy and life is full of hope. It required no great effort to repeat those thirteen simple words.

Three months into the cultivation of this new habit, he began to have dreams again.

In the first dream his wife, like the first drop of summer rain, descended on top of him. He advanced and she did not retreat. In the second dream he saw a ladder resting against the courtyard wall, and as he climbed it, the ladder automatically extended itself upwards. In the third dream (he was not sure if it was a dream or a memory that surfaced in a half awake state) his wife collapsed to the floor in the wake of their daughter's funeral. As he followed the small coffin he saw the petals of the white chrysanthemum by his daughter's face tremble, twitch and a thin streak of blood ooze out of the flower. In the fourth dream he returned to the campus where he first met his wife. He was in the graduating class and she was a freshman. He told her by the lake that he loved her and wished to marry her and have many children with her.

...

Five years after his daughter's death, his wife returned home with a little girl.

The girl was three years old. He planted a fig tree for her to celebrate her arrival, his saved marriage or something. The girl grew up, remembering nothing, and his wife did not tell her or him anything. He intended to tell her the story of her older sister who died young.

She died without any pain. Her eyes took after her mother's and her face resembled her father's. She had the temperament of a boy. Once her head crashed into a wall and she did not cry. Her parents took many pictures of her (he would show the younger girl those photographs). Look, she was just like you, very, very pretty, and like you she had almond-shaped eyes. Like you, she had a full forehead and freckles. She loved to hear stories, just like you do. What kind of stories? *The Little Red Riding Hood,* of course. She had long fingers. How long? This long. She had the swift legs of a fawn. She liked to kiss Daddy and Mommy just like you do. Come give Daddy a kiss.

It was on the tip of his tongue. He had rehearsed the details of his daughter's story so many times it was almost impossible to keep it bottled up any longer.

I had to do this for both our sakes.

For the sake of his wife and the little girl, so that they'd have a chance to fulfill those thirteen simple words, he could keep it bottled up.

The little girl grew into a big girl, although only in age. She had a small frame that invited tender affection but lacked sensuality. He still repeated three times to himself every day: I am all right. I am happy and life is full of hope. They decided not to reveal the truth about her birth to the girl. They tried to accomplish this in various ways, for example, by discouraging her from speaking to neighbors. They tried to make it difficult for her to make friends on their block. They told her that those kids that hung out together on their block might appear to have fun now, but decades from now they would find it not so funny. Or that given her smarts, she should focus on her school work. They enrolled her in an elementary school far from home, transporting her to and from school both in the morning and in the afternoon in two round trips every day, to make sure that no adults other than her parents had a chance to approach her. Every night they would check her book bag after she went to sleep as if it were the only place where a girl's secrets were kept. They were afraid that someone might take her away from them.

In middle school, she started boarding at the school. She got good grades and enjoyed good health, at least she did not suffer from any major illness that required surgery. She had good looks. While her hair was not black enough, and her lips were not red enough, she had regular, well-balanced features. He wondered sometimes what his own daughter would look like if she had lived to this age.

One Friday, she came home from school to tell them she intended to cut her long hair short. "Are you sure you want it so short? It's not a style becoming a girl. You are not that tall and the close-cut hair would make you look like a little boy," his wife tried to dissuade her. "Long on hair, but short on brains."

"Long hair absorbs all the nutrients that are needed for mental acuity and that would interfere with my studies," the girl countered.

The girl's decision caused his wife endless anxiety that night, so he tried to comfort her. "It's not a big deal."

"But don't you find it a little odd?" She asked. "Don't be silly," he said. "She just wants to focus on her school work."

The next day the girl got herself a crew cut and he was positive with his comment. "Not bad, it makes you look sharp." "Well, you have a small face, so on the whole it looks fine on you," his wife managed to echo his positivity.

"I find it quite handsome on me," the girl said. "This style suits me well." But after looking them in their eyes, she demanded, "If you don't find it pretty on me at all, then is it really pretty?"

"It looks fine to us," he reassured her.

"What if it is really quite ugly and only you think it is pretty?"

"Then at least you'll have our votes," his wife answered. "If it turns out that most people think otherwise, you can always let it grow back."

"Forget it," she said. "I think this hairstyle is fine."

When she was 16, she learned to sew in her arts and crafts class. She later joined a hobby group devoted to dress design. From then on, she refused to wear any dress that she didn't pick herself.

At 17, they found a book with the title "Sexual Physiology" in her book bag. His wife held the book out to him. "Don't you find it odd that she can read this kind of books?"

"You're right, we would never read this kind of books ..."

"There's something odd about this book," his wife interrupted him. "I can't believe you don't find it odd. Don't you find her so different from us? Well, I suppose it is determined by her genes after all."

All these years he had never asked his wife about the circumstances surrounding the arrival of the girl. Now that he had finally been let in on the truth, he found it strange that his wife had made the decision years ago to adopt this out-of-wedlock child of a young woman working in a hair salon.

In this light, the many things that happened to her later became easier to comprehend. Of course, they had never had the heart to tell her that they were not her biological parents.

By the time she reached 18, she had developed a unique charm. The summer when she finished taking the college entrance examination, she sat in front of her mirror and devised a whole system of coquettish expressions and body language. "I refused to accept them, but also let them know that I had not ignored them." "A consummate lover is the loneliest, saddest person." "One should be good at flirting. Affection is a tangled skein of multicolored threads and flirting helps to tease them apart so that one can enjoy the colorfulness. Flirting is a kaleidoscope through which finite affection appears like a many-splendored thing." Such were some of the many observations in her diary.

"Daddy, do you really love me?" She asked one morning as she ate her porridge. His wife had left for her workout and there were only the two of them in the house.

"Of course," he answered as he watered the flowers on the balcony.

"Why?"

"Because I am your father."

"Does it mean then if you were not my father you would not love me?"

"If I were not your father, I would probably not even know you."

"If you were not my father and you got to know me, would you love me?"

"What makes you ask a question like that?"

"I want everybody to love me."

He often recalled this conversation with sadness, and each time he did so the sadness deepened. It was a sadness shared by the two of them—the sadness of not receiving love, and of not being able to give love. She was like a drowning person, her arms flailing as she struggled to clutch at a rope. Every love affair was a hopeful struggle of life itself, because only such struggles alone could confirm to her that she was alive.

The first time she tasted the bitter fruit of disappointed love, he happened to be home to see her walk in glum-faced and spend the entire afternoon at the table contemplating the red dracaena in a vase.

"Why are you looking at it?" He asked.

"I like its color, such a festive dark red."

She had brought her face very close to the

bouquet, her nose touching the long, slender leaves. Then he saw her tongue dart out to lick at the leaves.

"But it does not taste red." She pressed her face down into her crossed arms. "There's no more red in my life, Dad."

Do I love her? He had come to the gradual realization that she was everything that the daughter he had in mind was not. She would never receive his unconditional love. But as if to compensate for this reservation, he seemed to be constantly manufacturing love in his heart, so that at least it would be perceived as a love that was full and whole. He remembered buying picture storybooks for her and obtaining a reputedly effective talisman to protect her from evil spirits, and he never once administered corporal punishment to her. If I told her, I don't love you. I can't love you like a father should. What would be her reaction? Yes, it's true that I don't love you. I don't love you because you smile flirtatiously at everybody, because you spend an inordinate amount of time writing frivolous fiction, because you are picky about food, because you are stubbornly convinced you are always right. I don't love you because you are not my biological daughter. You could never hope to surpass she that had existed before, but you nonetheless have been my life for the last dozen years.

One late night when he was in bed it suddenly occurred to him that she was really very smart and pretty and that he had never told her he was proud of her. On an impulse, he got up and went to her room. A soft light filtered out at the bottom of her door and he knocked.

When he walked in, he nearly tripped over her. It was much, much later before life went back to normal.

He would always remember the look on her face. He tried to picture how she had clutched at her chest before she sank into unconsciousness. He tried to imagine what he would feel after gulping down a whole bottle of pills—or maybe not feel anything. He thought maybe he should accept fate and come to terms with his loss so that there would be no further losses. He could start from tomorrow on to be a good father, a father who could truly say to himself, "I am all right, I am happy and life is full of hope." In the dark, he stared at the ceiling.

I love you. I am your father.

The girl discovered afterwards that there was no

poetry in suicide. She had been sure that she would die and that it would remain a mystery. But then everybody saw it and knew what happened, and the mystery was gone.

In the wake of the incident, the girl bought herself a large black shawl. She would pace the rooms carrying it with her. Sometimes she would drape it over her head and at other times she would wrap it around her body like a shroud. In the end, she tacked the thing to the window to keep out the sunlight.

He decided to have a talk with his daughter.

"It was a stupid act," he told her. "The next time you contemplate suicide, try to do it after my death. Then I would have no control over it. Don't ever do it again when I am alive."

She bowed her head. "I won't. Death does not yet become me."

Why did you do this? He was strongly tempted to ask her. But then it occurred to him that she might resent the question and counter in her heated voice, why do we need this discussion? So he fell silent. Then he started to say something conciliatory, but gave up after a few tries.

"I'll figure it out myself, Dad," she said, signaling

him to leave her alone.

The afternoon before the incident, she picked out a long white dress with matching white braided shoulder straps. She was worried that the long skirt would pick up dirt from the dusty street. She wore it to meet with the man she had loved for a long time. She had given herself to him a while back. It had been her idea—in memory of a lead singer in a band who had died of a bullet. Afterwards, he started to evade her, before explicitly asking to break off with her. But that didn't stop her from wanting to see him.

When she pushed the door open, her skirt caught an empty liquor bottle. The man was lying on the floor stone drunk. Her white skirt lost its brightness the moment she entered the room. She lay down next to him. They were locked in an embrace, fondling each other, their fingers exploring and their legs intertwined. There was in her heart room only for him. Her skirt began to crease and bunch up. He was now on top of her, sinking into her all the way. With every thrust, her breasts swung sideways like windswept water in a basin.

It was then that his friends walked in.

He slowed down, as though to allow the spectators to follow with their eyes the trajectory of the piston's motion. Someone turned on the music. A steady stream flooded in. The man finally completed his one-man show. She cleaned herself up with a McDonald's paper napkin that had been used to wipe off someone's mouth. She didn't know why she did it. Someone else had crouched down beside her by this time and started to tug at her. The skirt conveniently had no buttons to be laboriously unfastened. It was an afternoon of wide-flung legs, an afternoon of burning desire, of spent energy and flagging interest and disgust. Between bouts of an obscure dull ache, she gulped down mouthfuls of liquor until she puked. I am here. They used me in a crazed rampage. Why do they call sexual intercourse making love? How can true love be made? Sex is a continuous passage through darkness. No matter, I am still alive. Ignore them. Ignore them. These words bombarded her mind throughout that afternoon.

An hour and a half later, all the men were spent. There was no bleeding, but she walked with some difficulty, although the difficulty was not apparent. The ache in the vagina was of course invisible. The sensation reminded her of a certain "most beautiful" hostess at a Shanghai Expo pavilion, who was mobbed by visitors asking to have their admission tickets stamped by her and to have pictures taken with her. A burning sensation remained in her eyes even when she looked away from the one-per-second flashes of the cameras.

When she limped back into the street, she felt like a hundred and twenty years old. She returned to her own room, removed the white dress, changed into her pajamas and walked into the bathroom. The hot water had a damp smell, a smell of something that had dried and then gotten wet again and dried again and gotten wet yet again. For some reason tears did not come to her eyes. Her body fluids had apparently been banished, wave upon wave, to some deeper recesses.

She was twenty that year. She had desired to marry that man, to create a child with him, to love their child, sing to him or her, and teach him or her to read. Now, all that had become a mirage staring at her from a great distance.

She felt much better after taking a bath. In fact, she felt no pain of any sort. She had no sensation, really. And yet she felt like crying, crying uncontrollably, but on reflection found it strange and affected. Then she tried to smile, but why? Could it be that she was glad that she had been violated? She was at a loss as to what to do next.

She was medicated and her stomach was pumped. The first thing she did after her recovery was weep. Weeping turned out to be a new experience for her, and she never wept again after that.

For a period, she had a strong urge to see that man. She rehearsed time and time again the anticipated dialog.

"How could you hurt me so?"

"I didn't do it on purpose. You came to me on your own after I had already told you I no longer loved you."

"What?"

"I don't love you." He stepped out of her way. "I'm sorry."

Maybe some kind of body language was called for?

"Sorry," he said as he laid a hand on her shoulder.

"Don't touch me! Take your hand away!" She said in an icy tone. "You make me sick."

And she turned her face to the side and started

to puke, the vomit splashing on his shoes.

The scene was a little vulgar.

"I hate you," she said.

He sat down by her side. "I did love you once."

She averted her face, refusing to look at him. "No, you did not, you never did."

"I did, but I was unable to love only you." He told her. "I am very sorry about what happened the other day."

"It was a horrible thing ..."

"I know," he said.

"I just wanted you to know this. I know you'll never be able to feel the horror that I felt."

"What do you wish me to do?" His hand came to rest on her shoulder and started to inch downward and forward. "Do you still want to be with me?"

She drew back to escape his caress. "I don't think that's possible. How would those friends of yours think of me, or of you, for that matter?"

"I don't think that matters at all."

"They would think I'm a tramp."

"Don't say that."

"They defiled me because they considered me already used."

"It's not true."

"They thought I was dirty because you no longer loved me."

"I can't love only one woman."

Lying in bed, she yanked the black shawl off the window and draped it over her face. As she breathed, the shawl rippled as if it had a life of its own.

He doesn't love you and still you offered yourself to him. You have no self-respect. What? So she repeated it to herself once more. He doesn't love you and still you offered yourself to him. You have no self-respect. Then she repeated it a third time.

At that moment she experienced for the first time the sensation of weightlessness, of disorientation and of having been dealt a body blow. Before that, she was like a top whipped into a frenzied spin, but now the spinning had come to an abrupt stop.

She sat up, picked up the shawl that had slipped to the floor and put it into a drawer. She crossed to the window and opened it. She thought she had made a big mess of her life. From now on, she needed to get her act together and start over.

"Dad, do you still love me now that I made such a

mess of my life?" She asked.

"I love you," he answered. "You'll always be my beloved daughter."

"Mom, will you forgive me too?"

"I don't blame you. My heart goes out to you."

"I feel better now. I know I've let you down. I won't do anything ever again to break your hearts or cause you grief."

She did not mention the incident to friends, nor did she confide in her parents, believing that doing so would only bring contempt upon her. Even in her diary, perhaps expecting her parents to peek into it, she only wrote that nothing noteworthy happened today.

The day she ran into that man in the street a year later, her diary entry read: I memorized a lot of new English words today. I thought I would forget. But I did not forget.

A few days later: I drank too much coffee today. As a result I had trouble falling asleep. I am sure I will be able to fall asleep, and fast asleep.

In the years after that chance encounter, she caught

sight of him a number of times and maybe he also caught a glimpse of her a few times. They had no verbal contact at all.

At first, she tried to avoid going near his neighborhood. She chose to use streets that they had never taken together. She tried to deny his existence. But at the same time, she craved, in her dreams, to return to the scene of their first encounter and start over. In a warehouse, she watched him sing to his guitar. They noticed each other, they drank and chatted, they left the warehouse and he led her through street after street, across an urban garden. They walked on and on and on, and into a room, and were enveloped by darkness.

After two years, she was able to ignore his existence, and she was confident that they had finally become total strangers.

One afternoon, ten years later, she walked past him on her way to visit her parents. It was him who called out to her.

"Do you remember me?"

It took her a few seconds to remember.

They talked briefly before she walked into her parents' home. Mother was washing something in the kitchen. She stepped into her own room to find nothing had changed. The diary she kept as a young girl remained hidden beneath the mattress. The bed was neatly made. The books she had read still sat neatly against the wall. After inspecting her own room she surveyed the bathroom. There were no traces she had imagined would be there. Was it then really over?

She returned to the kitchen.

"What's the matter?" Her mother asked when she saw her appear at the doorway. Mother appeared to have aged a lot.

"Nothing," she answered.

"I'll fix you something to eat."

"Okay."

"Have some soup."

"Okay."

Mom, I suffered a great deal. She did not say it.

Mom, it's finally over. She did not say that either.

"Mom, this soup is so delicious," she said instead. "How did you make it?"

She got married when she was thirty-two.

She gave a detailed account to a close friend of her first kiss with her new man. She told the story with a smile. She said the room reeked of tobacco and liquor but he was odorless. I did not smell anything, not even bath lotion. His mouth gave off no noticeable odor, not overly clean, nor overly warm. It was plain breath. How is it possible that he did not smell of tobacco or liquor, or toothpaste? She repeated the rhetorical question twice to her close friend.

What about other details? She couldn't remember. Even the detail about his putting one of her plaits into his mouth and chewing on it eluded her memory. Was it because she had since cropped her hair?

Before the wedding she developed a fascination for wedding dress fabrics. The lustrous, beautiful charmeuse, organza, chiffon, satin, tulle and lace. They all looked so soft. She pictured herself draped in such a gown, sashaying through a vast virgin forest, the wedding train draped over brown twigs and green moss, a streak of light penetrating the dense, hanging branches and leaves.

But he vetoed her idea, dismissing a honeymoon in a forest as a sentimental whim. It would be so easy to get lost in a forest, and they would surely have to endure mosquitos, ticks, leeches and who knows what other pesky critters, even poisonous snakes, come to think of it. If there was a thunderstorm, they would have to worry about being struck by lightning. She wanted to explain but couldn't come up with any persuasive explanation.

She let him take her in his arms. "You silly girl. You have such silly, romantic ideas in your head. You need to be more practical!"

She was suddenly reminded of that man who could sing with his guitar, of a line he wrote for a song: Love is but a match burning itself out in the air. Not so, stupid! Not love. Love is a summer thunder shower, a prank played between good friends. Marriage is a match burning itself out in the air!

There was nothing out of the ordinary about their marriage, because they were both ordinary people. They went to work, came home and lounged about, one knitting, the other drinking beer, or one going out with friends to window shop and the other going out for a beer with friends. Some nights they made love. They got along pretty well, although occasional bickering was inevitable. As life dragged on like this, she thought about keeping a cat. He was against it, because he believed cat claws would mar their furniture.

"We can train it so that it will behave and leave the furniture alone," she suggested.

"It has nothing to do with training. Cats claw furniture."

"Then we can get a wood stick exclusively for its clawing pleasure," she said.

"But that may encourage its clawing."

She had a strong urge to let out a shriek, a shriek to split the ears, just as a cat would split the grain of furniture wood with its claws. Of course, she never tried it. She figured nothing would have come of it even if she had tried.

Eventually their bickering subsided because whenever there was an irreconcilable difference of opinion, he would smile tolerantly. "You are probably suffering from PMS."

Her PMS symptoms began to appear earlier, about three weeks before menstruation. When she didn't care to discuss a question or wanted to avoid an argument over something, she would warn him. "I'm starting to have PMS symptoms."

"Oh really? I thought you just had your menstruation."

"You're wrong," she corrected him. "Menstruation can start anytime."

Possibly befuddled by what was going on, he began to come home very late at night. Or did he go somewhere to have drinks with people who knew more about these things?

She never waited for him to come home, not caring how much he drank in town. She would take her evening walks alone, carrying a plastic bag filled to capacity with cat food. As she sauntered past the flower beds in the residential compound, she'd spot many cats lounging indolently and others that were on the contrary too leery of humans to invite affection. She only caressed kittens. They meowed so insistently for her attention she simply had to pick every one of them up.

One evening, she watched spellbound by a pair of cats, one on top of the other, engaged in an intimate act in the moonlight. The caterwauling of those cats in heat reminded her of the cries of Rosemary's Baby.

That evening she examined herself closely in the bathroom mirror. Her dark eyes protruded a little because of her myopia. The first crow's feet had appeared under her eyes. She had a beautifully shaped but not flirtatious mouth. In short, she had the face of a reserved introvert. Was this look of hers the reason for his cooling towards her?

She woke in the dark to find her cheeks streaked with tears. The tears must have trickled from the corners of her eyes into her ears. The small clock on the night table ticked away. An octopus was known to pick winners. Everyone knows about this octopus in Germany that could predict the winner of sport matches. What animal could forecast her happiness?

She turned her face to look in his direction, to see if he happened to be awake also. But he had his eyes closed and was breathing evenly. She reached over to hold his hand in hers.

She intended to inform him the very next morning that she was going on a long trip, her destination a forest.

"Do you know your way around where you are going?" He asked.

"It's not a problem. I will do my research online, do my homework well before I leave."

"Why do you want to go there?" He continued his probing.

"I'm not doing it for any particular reason."

"It is a long way from home," he said.

"I feel I need to go."

"I understand," he finally relented.

It was decided then. She would leave in the spring when the flowers start to bloom. She would bring a portable tent, some medicine, a Swiss Army knife, a flashlight and a raincoat for this trip into the forest.

What did she wish to see in the forest?

In fact, the first night she would see a young man in a white shirt and jeans. His tent was pitched not far from her. He sat there on the water-resistant mat at the opening of his tent, his legs crossed and his hands clasped over his knee.

Would something start between them?

There was only silence. She passed her fingers through her hair a few times, to arrange it neatly behind her ears. Once she lifted her left hand to adjust the strap of her bra over her right shoulder. She cast a bold glance in his direction, but he remained impassive. Finally, feeling the discomfort of her sitting posture maintained for such a long time, she bade a silent goodbye and withdrew into her own little space and zipped up her tent.

What about the second day?

It would be spent walking about in this

unfamiliar place, lying down face up on the grass to rest whenever she was tired. The winding trail meandered through dense scrub. Occasionally she would see an open clearing in the woods inundated by sunlight.

Did she wear her long dress with its hem reaching all the way to the ground?

Guess!

How would we know?

Take a guess! I can't help you.

Well then, we'll let her continue on her way.

So she walked on. The forest was so densely populated by trees that the sun became shifting bits in a kaleidoscope. Leaves rustled underfoot and parted like lake water cleaved by a boat. Occasional twigs brushed against her clothes. The long, lonely walk dampened her spirits. She had a momentary longing for her husband to suddenly appear before her. Of course, nothing of that kind would happen. After a few minutes she began to loathe herself for missing her husband. But her thoughts abruptly turned to the first night they spent together. They each held in their arms a body that they did not yet realize they would in time come to detest. She recalled that he did not close the bedroom window that night and the window drapes billowed in soft changing lines in the breeze as he held her hands tightly, and from time to time leaned over to kiss her on the face and the neck. All these details must have their meaning in one's memory, don't they?

And what happened after that?

After that, a shower ruined her plan to enjoy a leisurely picnic under the balmy spring sun. The ground instantly turned muddy and she had to be extra careful when she walked. She decided to sit down under the shelter of a big tree and enjoy the view around her—the glistening drops of rainwater clinging to the leaves, a patch of wild flowers in full bloom under the tree, the slate gray clouds overhead and the foliage turned a fresh tender green by the rain. Those details all seemed interesting and intrigued her.

She is not in a good mood?

No, there's nothing wrong with her mood.

But she appears to be in low spirits.

Her mood's not that different from her usual mood, not great but not bad either.

She is moody.

Why are you so keen to see her depressed and

moody?

Because she has no idea what happiness is, so nothing can make her happy.

Does she still have the possibility of feeling happy?

She needs to know what she wants. Family? Children? Comfortable life? An untrammeled inner life?

These are only part of an enjoyable life.

Yes. Happiness can sometimes simply mean a glitch in life.

Do we then still need her to continue her voyage?

Why not?

The weather cleared after the rain. She felt a new calm. She even had an urge to take out her cell phone to write a few lines of verse. But then she blamed herself for not showing a greater interest in the natural scenery around her. She made the right decision in taking this trip, she thought with a smile of self-approbation flickering across her face. But her light mood did not last when she noticed a few condoms hanging on the top branch of a shrub. They were yellowing and flaccid, clearly from heavy use.

In the evening she was in for another shock. The

young man she had tried to seduce the previous night had once again pitched tent not far from her. But this evening his behavior surprised her. He walked toward her holding two cans, a smile playing on his face. She realized they were two cans of beer. She accepted one graciously and immediately opened it to take a sip.

"You are out here alone?" He asked.

"Yes."

"You are not from this area."

"No, I come from afar."

"How far?"

She gestured vaguely with her hand. She didn't have to go out of her way to be polite. She could now examine his face up close. It was not a face that appealed to her. He invited her over to his tent, which was clearly much bigger than hers. She was reluctant, but he insisted. Finally she agreed, but was privately disappointed with herself for not knowing how to say no. To ease her nervousness, she kept sipping her beer. As she drank more, her ability to control her nods and smiles were gradually impaired.

The light was ebbing, but she was still sober enough to remind herself that she was only paying a short social call in this tent. A muffled boom pierced the quiet. It occurred to her at this precise moment that it must have some kind of significance. It was followed by intermittent thunderclaps. She thought afterwards that the sound probably represented the ominous rumbling long suppressed in her body, an angry roar of something trying to shake free from some shackles. It just happened to coincide with a meteorological phenomenon.

Violent thrusting and shaking accompanied the rattling of thunder.

When thunder and rain ceased, she was again seized by an uneasy feeling. She regretted not having brought a compass for the trip, for if she had done so she would not have gone astray in this place. What was she doing in someone else's tent? She fled back to her own little space. The next day when she opened her tent door, the sun was already up. Her tent was the only one in sight.

She stopped short in front of a shrub not far from her tent. At the sight of that long, limp grayish piece of natural latex, the look that she had contrived at the start of the trip of composure and joyful contemplation of nature was driven from her face.

She did not regain her composure for the rest

of the day. The trail was indeed harder than usual to negotiate that day and she even slipped once on the lichen and had a bad fall, scratching her calf on the gravel by the trail. To stop the bleeding, she cut a long band of fabric from her white silk skirt to bind the wound.

She can surely now be allowed to end her voyage?

Yes, I think she should now feel more sure of herself and more true to herself.

Are you sure she will know what she should do next?

She can wake up now. She will get pregnant. Pills, condoms, she has no use for them now. What she needs now is a child.

Carrying a secret that would never be revealed, even to the day of her death, she willed herself to become part of her husband's life, or of their married life. She cooked breakfast for him every morning, washed his clothes and went obediently to bed with him every night. Their bedroom now reverberated with billing and cooing, alternating with peals of laughter. They talked about how wonderful it would be to have a child of their own. They had decided ahead of time what skills their child was going to possess. Even before she got pregnant, she already started to worry about the labor pains that would come in waves.

They did not yet know that the child would eventually become a piece of fiction, leaving no trace except in the form of faded, yellowed photos. Anyway, they once firmly believed that the child would always be there. Something went wrong along the way.

Life went on like this until about the third year, when a fly changed everything.

That afternoon she returned to her parents' home for a visit.

"Are you still unable to get pregnant?" Her mother asked as they sat in the living room making small talk.

"I'm taking traditional medicines."

As she started to give an account of the different things they'd tried, a fly flew into the room, first harassing the chandelier before diving to buzz about her face. She was telling her mother that someone helpfully suggested that they try baby dog meat cooked with black beans. How annoying the fly is! It just won't leave me in peace. As she talked, she heard an inner voice on a dual track accompanied by the constant hum of the fly: Do I really need a baby? Do

I really need a baby by him?

"Mom, I don't think I really want a child," she blurted out. "I am doing it for my own needs. I am lonely and a child could fill that void."

I live in a rut and I feel so lonely. Some stains on one's clothes can never be removed. If I have a child, I will no longer need him. Isn't this a good enough reason to want a child? Why should today be different from yesterday or tomorrow? I can become a good mother. You both have faith in me, don't you? Put it in my womb! Let it be with me.

The fly continued its buzzing. She said something completely different from the above to her parents.

"A child is a life. Maybe I'm not ready for it yet? I really have little knowledge of life itself. Is this a hint from the heavens that I don't have what it takes to have a child of my own?"

She noticed the momentary reaction of disbelief from her parents. She never noticed that the fly had left the room.

Her mother swayed ever so slightly in her chair. Her father's hands tightened their grip on the arms of his chair.

"We must ..."

Must what, Mom?

"We can't ..."

Can't what, Dad?

Her mother suddenly excused herself, saying she didn't feel well and needed to go upstairs to lie down with her head propped against her pillow.

"Dad, did I say something wrong?"

Her father tried to put her mind at ease. "Don't worry, it's not serious. It comes with age."

Yes, what really matters is not the sudden malaise of mother, but ...

"Must ..." She tried to remind her father by murmuring the word.

Her father rose form his chair to make some tea. "Yes, we must put our mind to it and help find a solution to your problem."

Must and can't.

That night she had a dream in which she wriggled out of the body of a woman. Someone held her up and presented her to that woman—a stranger. The woman in turn handed her to another woman, who was her mother. She heard her mother say, thank you, you gave me the gift of life, a hope. Her mother held her in her arms and brought her home. It must be a late afternoon, with the light ebbing. In the night she lay in bed and watched mother and father make love. She heard father tell mother how much he loved her. Mother had a beautiful body. She suddenly started to cry. Father laid his hands on her body for the first time. It was a pair of callous hands, every welted vein telling a story of weariness and sadness. Those trembling hands picked her up, rocking her. She saw only the back of her mother, who was already fast asleep on her side. Father raised her to the height of his shoulders, his mouth puckered, approaching her ear, as if to tell her a secret. Mother shifted her weight in the bed. Father's lips brushed past her ear to fall on her cheek.

Dreams impassively hide all. They unreservedly tell all.

That summer morning when she woke from the dream, it was quieter than usual. Perhaps because it was still very early. She went to the kitchen to pour a glass of water and surveyed the space in front of her eyes, her back leaning against the sink. The kitchen was not very spacious, but it was neat and clean. Her eyes fell on the fresh cut flowers in a vase on the dining table. The glass panes on the cabinets, while not dazzlingly shiny, were passably bright. The urban noise rose as the city stirred from its sleep, with doors and windows opening and closing, and birds chirping.

Every morning resembled another. In half an hour her husband would get up from bed, make himself presentable and sit down at the dining table, with his legs slightly apart, waiting for her to bring his breakfast, drinking his glass of milk before leaving, looking fully ready to take on the world.

The evening routine never changed either. The TV was forever on. They were law-abiding citizens who always sorted their trash into the various categories for disposal, and they were interested in what went on in society and in their community. Sometimes he would start to talk about her effort at getting pregnant, referring to some unique treatment suggested by a colleague. She listened as she put leftovers into containers and did the dishes. And just when she wanted very much to be left alone, she would ask him if he was interested in doing something together with her. He would invariably answer in the affirmative.

After having her glass of water, she left the

kitchen to go into the bathroom. She took off her pajamas before the mirror. Her skin seemed to have slackened a little more compared to the previous year. She felt she had lost some kind of equilibrium in her body. The words of a girlfriend suddenly sprang to mind, to the effect that life would be better without change. She imagined sometimes that she'd receive a phone call informing her of an accident in which her husband was hit by a speeding car on his way to work (or on his way home). There would be an ambulance, policemen and the driver of the car involved. She would be distraught with grief. There would follow the funeral, wreaths, friends' condolences and words of sympathy. Of course, it could perfectly be the other way around and she would have no objection. She was not afraid of death at all. She imagined the moment of being hit herself by a car. Everything would be over in a flash. She would be totally free. Why not make it a late afternoon, preferably in autumn twilight, after a light shower, the pavement damp with recent rain, the neon lights and car headlights reflecting off its surface. There would be a traffic jam and passersby would gather to gawk, some snapping pictures with their cell phones. Her data would be erased completely from the system. Someone would notify her husband. How would he dispose of her personal effects? He would have to pay a visit to her parents and notify some of her friends. How long would he wait before he would feel the need to find another woman? This was one thing she had a hard time imagining.

"After living for a hundred years, everyone will die." She watched him as she said it. She didn't really mean to say it because it might create a problem, but the words just rolled off her tongue in spite of it.

He appeared tired but went on reading the financial pages, although somewhat astonished. "What did you say?"

"The sun will always shine brightly. The stores will always be open for business. Children will go to school. But we, including our future child, will all die someday, leaving not a trace, as if nothing had ever happened."

"Is something wrong with you?"

She did not reply to the question.

"Don't you want a child anymore?" He leaned forward, an expression of surprise coming into his face. "I thought you've always liked children."

"Yes, children are such adorable creatures. They inspire hope."

"Then you ..."

She crossed to the window and opened it.

"I changed my mind not long ago." She said. "I don't know why, but I just don't want to make a superhuman effort against nature anymore."

"Have you thought of consulting me before making the decision?"

"It is not a big deal. Nothing would change. I just don't feel like forcing myself."

"Don't you want a lovely little baby?"

"Of course I do ..." she said. "But I have a strange feeling that intercourse is all we do ... it shouldn't be like this."

After turning off the light that night, she lay awake for a long time. Her husband had gone back to his parents' apartment. She got up from the bed and opened the window drapes, allowing some light to come into the room, which seemed to bring some relief.

The daily routine remained unchanged for her. She cleaned the apartment, went to the supermarket to get her groceries and bought a few DVDs. The stories in those DVD movies seemed to have more reality than her own life, as if the more phantasmagoric the pictorial images were, the more realistic they were, as if her life was a mere imitation of the movies with a cheap movie set.

Her husband came home after only two nights. As he had always done, he sat at the dining table reading his paper, went out with his briefcase clutched under his armpit, and on weekends he would lie in for some extra hours of sleep. They made love occasionally, although it was no longer an affair entailing much sweating, or anger, or thrill. They felt neither full of energy nor drained physically or emotionally. Both of them tried to maintain normalcy and hide their heads in the sand or sweep problems under the rug. Up to the moment they agreed on a divorce, they treated each other with unfailing courtesy. Only, one or the other would sometimes get out of bed in the dark, thinking the other was asleep, and quietly crossed the unlit living room to the kitchen or the bathroom at the other end of their home.

A year later they parted amicably. He paused several times as he was packing his stuff. He didn't have much in the way of personal effects: a few souvenirs from sightseeing trips, which he stared at blankly. They were still in love when they bought those together. In some pictures taken of them next to each other, the two lovers destined to eventually part ways smiled brilliantly in a cloudless setting. There were some books on the stock market, some clothes and shoes. A chord was struck somewhere. Either she took him in her arms or he took her in his arms. Neither remembered who took the first step.

They let the impulse run its course.

They lay in bed with their shoulders touching. "I don't understand, really, how we have come to this?" he said, opening his eyes and staring at the ceiling.

"Neither do I," she said, propping herself up on her elbows and examining him. "I don't even understand myself. I don't know what I want, what I can ask for ..."

"It's a pity ..." he said in a low voice. "I wish I knew."

They stayed a while longer in that position. Neither said anything more. Then he left lugging his suitcase. She stood at the window, watching him melt into the crowd in the street and disappear from view.

Nine months later she gave birth to a baby girl.

Thirty-One Days of Love

Day 1

She was a 32-year-old editor of a literary magazine. For a few years, she had tried her hand at writing and submitting her manuscripts to publishers, but that had been a discouraging experience. She was discouraged and she liked to discourage her authors. She was also a notoriously finicky editor. She thought of herself as a latecomer. The idealism and impulses of the eighties ignited a splendor of words, but she was not born until 1978. Her adolescence was faintly tinged by rock and roll and she grew up familiar with the scent of marijuana, but Wei Hui, who graduated five classes before her, already published her *Shanghai Baby*. She was always a step behind.

She was in a good mood that evening. When waiting to log onto MSN, she tried to recall his face but couldn't. Memory is such a mystery! Some faces simply elude definition. Could it be that when the soul is dominant the physical can only be a spiritual rather than a formal likeness? Rough and unrefined, she hit on this description after much mental searching. Rough and unrefined, blurred, gloomy, drawn inward, with contours but no outlines, the face vaguely suggested a plantless twilit wasteland illuminated in spots by a faint light of unknown provenance.

She felt a flicker of excitement, a kind of readiness.

Day 2

His inbox:

That was a pleasant and unexpected conversation we had at the conference. Is there any way it can be resumed more privately and at more leisure? I know you are a busy person.

Did you not find it as strange as I did that we immediately understand each other so well? For we did understand each other uncommonly well, did we not? Or is this perhaps a product of the overexcited brain of a quondam literary youth (a term coined in the 1980's in China to denote a young person with literary aspirations but no formal education)? Should tangled emotions, tortuous like some esoteric verses, be revealed in all their clarity?

Your discussion, ranging over a number of topics, including monologues in novels, the rambling running style of prose writing, and the expression of passion in irony, intrigued me. You mentioned your intention to write a novel devoted to the communication of thoughts and feelings. I am sure it will be rich in creative ideas. You asked what I thought. I said it was an interesting idea and suggested you find a real life person with whom to communicate so that the novel would gain in vividness with the input of two souls. You asked if I was game. Was that a formal invitation?

Although that novel may still be up in the air at this time, my imagination has been stoked.

He was an ad agency copywriter, a renowned book reviewer, and an avid student of books that have won literary awards (the Prix Goncourt, the Man Booker Prize, the Nobel Prize, the Akutagawa Prize, the Pulitzer Prize). In high school, he considered becoming a librarian. Once introduced to the mindboggling variety of genres and styles of world literature, he had periods of grandiose dreams of writing something that would earn a place in it, which was always followed by dejection and low self-esteem. He didn't have any confidence in his own capacity to contribute to or change this grand edifice. He wrote poems in his youth, imagined the critical comments on them, and decided to keep the collection in deep storage on his computer, showing it only to a girl met recently. In his book reviews he employed a fine style that incorporated the parenthetical and parallel montage of the Nouveau Roman and the equivocation and impenetrability of translated American writing course materials, unintelligible even when read ten times. As of late, he had been invited to sundry seminars sponsored by major publishers. Attendance at these events typically begins to thin out fifteen minutes into them. He would firmly fix his frail frame to his armchair and shrewdly keep his own counsel. Let those university professors wax eloquent and let them pronounce their self-assured judgments so that he could subsequently demonstrate, in writing, his own synthesizing, balancing, and analytic brilliance. He knew all too well how to graft one thing onto another and saw value where value was. So he chooses to be silent. If called upon to speak, all he had to do was point out a few places where the book was found wanting. He derived other benefits from this second occupation of his: a continuous supply of new books for him to read, fees paid for his articles sent from all corners of the country, travel expenses in cash stuffed in small envelopes of different colors, the opportunity to know new comers.

His regular job consisted of writing copy for a Japanese ad agency. His portfolio of projects waxes and wanes with time. Keeping his clients happy was a cakewalk for him. He cuts and pastes feature articles in fashion magazines before redistribution to his clientele. The risk of being found out is nil because the variability of words and phrases is infinite. His work whets his appetite for all kinds of information and knowledge—astrology, the study of blood types, Arabian perfumes, the state of AIDS in Africa, angels and Tantric Buddhism, the guillotine and the origin of witchcraft, Marquis de Sade and Sapph. Can these be considered knowledge? Wikipedia is like the heads of the Hydra.

A question that has been on his mind a lot lately is how a person finds, enters, and leaves another person's life. Every choice changes the final outcome. The analysis of a relationship can only be carried out after it is ended, like those *CSI* episodes, by poring over bits of hair, an argument, or an unidentified fingerprint. Is affection nurtured for affection's sake or for one's own sake? How will a passionate exterior with an indifferent interior affect the evolution of the other's affection?

After a period of practicing total self-effacement, he realized that all his emotions and his language had become none other than projections of the other, a mirror image of the other's emotions. He accepted and discovered the fascinations of the other and shared the other's pain and suffering. It all seemed quite meaningless, for he was now in thrall to his emotions. He felt like a superb fake whose exquisite moments were fleeting. He decided it was time to take a different tack.

9 a.m. to 6 p.m., Monday to Friday. He rode his bicycle to work in the early mornings, though he walked if the weather was nice. If he left home between 8:35 and 8:40, he would see a beauty walking on the sidewalk of Sinan Road. He followed her once and found that she would invariably enter that building located at the intersection of Ruijin Road and Jianguo Road West. He always passed her outside the wall of Ruijin Hospital on Jiande Road. It was a very long street with steam sometimes rising from the pavement. The morgue of the hospital was only steps away from

Sinan Road. If he wanted to see her, all he had to do was leave home and ride by in that time interval when she unfailingly appears, never earlier or later.

Nothing exciting happens on his way home from work shortly after 6 p.m. He locked his bike and climbed the two flights of wooden stairs to his own room. From all the windows of his room, he saw nothing but different perspectives of his residential compound, which boasted a garden. He, at the midpoint of his life and recently the object of desire of a lady editor, lived with a black cat in this old western-style house. The air was fresh in his room because he always left the window at the far end opened. The words "neat" and "cluttered" would not spring to mind if one were to describe the room. The residential compound itself was quiet but the corridors resonated with the unceasing noise of foot traffic.

He turned on the TV, braised a fish, plunked a bottle of rice wine on the table, and began his supper in front of his computer. He half-heartedly opened his inbox.

He didn't know what to think for a few seconds after reading it. Then he relaxed completely.

The black cat came over to him and he stroked

its back, imagining for a second it was her back he was stroking.

Later that night he opened his inbox to reread the email. The sender was clearly expecting an immediate reply. What could he give her? What would it be like to be with her? He figured he would have to make time for the relationship. But why pass up an opportunity to understand another person's journey of the heart? He would make it a drawn-out process in which he would cleverly compose his words, with deliberation, and watch, unobserved, the ups and downs, twists and turns of the other, occasionally throwing in some explicit, direct language so that she would stumble in the dark into those words that embroider affection. It would add drama and animation to the process.

A letter is but the first salvo. Now what song and dance should his fingers perform on the keyboard?

Day 3

Her inbox:

I agree with you. You were quiet and reticent at first, but when we started to discuss novels, you became animated. You talked about Rushdie, "that unrivaled talent" and "the equally gifted Angela Carter." You seem to have a particular softness for a certain briskness of writing? I was amazed by the expression on your face when you talked about them. It was one of enthusiasm—quite engaging. We also discussed the so-called dialogue style of writing. You brought up "the dialogue of souls" (someone joined the discussion at this point and talked about the mysteries of constellations). I believe in the power of the soul. I believe that the imaginative space of a novel is enriched by the inner lives of its characters, and it is possible even that the inner lives of the characters would elude the author's (a poetic, bizarre loss of control). Does this view hold sufficient attraction for you?

One paragraph. There was just that one paragraph!

"I agree with you." What does it mean? It could be he agreed that "we had a pleasant and unexpected conversation" or that "we did understand each other uncommonly well." Four simple words, yet she couldn't fathom his real thought. She examined every word with the eye of a fastidious editor in an attempt to find the meaning behind them. "Sufficient attraction," but the subject of the sentence was "this view." Was it a tacit encouragement of a meeting? She decided to react from her gut.

Even so, it was not easy to make up her mind. Snatches of plain, banal words filed past her mind's eye and faded. Why do so many people see fit to describe a love affair, an experience, men, women, and the body? One is rendered speechless and then forgets everything the moment one finishes reading the book. She had a sudden impulse to pay him an unannounced visit. Let him have a taste of her impulsiveness! Talking about impulse, it was a small black and white photo taken an eternity ago. Preferably, the weather should be rainy. The face should be pale to the point of translucency because of a long wait. The little heart, yet unprotected, covered with fine, delicate veinings. She couldn't resist going into the bathroom to look in the mirror.

Today she had on a loose-fitting white woolen sweater, which was new and therefore more eye-catching than her own person. She folded her arms cruciform over her chest, a hand clasped crosswise on each shoulder, so that she appeared to be hidden in her sweater. She should put her head ever so slightly on one side—it would add an engaging look of innocence.

But she could not escape the observation that she was in decline. She had to hide her full forehead behind a curtain of bangs because of the wrinkles. She tentatively opened her mouth a crack. The teeth were passably regular. With looks like these was it any wonder he couldn't instantly make up his mind about her? She was, after all, an ordinary woman—a prudish, dull woman editor.

But when she tried to recall his face, she was equally unable to form a clear picture of his features. It meant that he wasn't exactly cut an eye-catching figure. So they were even now. They were both of them kept outside the door, in the shadows, unable to recognize each other and unnoticed by others. But she recalled he was tall, not egregiously so, but tall enough to make him stoop his shoulders. She also recalled his style of dress, which had, for lack of a better description, something stale and limp about it. He wore a shirt, a knit sweater, a jacket, jeans, and casual shoes, looking overall no different than other men. He might not realize it, but there was something that bowed him down. She did not want to cast doubt on her power of observation, she prided herself on her eye for detail. Was it his complexion? The uneven sallow and swarthy tones of his skin blurred his facial features, and the unevenness cost him an air of poise and self-possession. Even when accompanied by a constant smile, his face had a high-strung quality to it. It struck her that she was fortunate to be a woman, because she was always able to radiate a perfect glow with the help of liquid foundation and compact powder, and no one could guess what was underneath the protective sheen.

I am intrigued by your views (the truth is I am interested in you). It gives me great pleasure that you are willing to share them with me (I can't wait to be asked out by you). This kind of reply appears to be a little contrived. How does one appear unflustered without being ambiguous? Given her flat, unexciting body and her straightjacketed, unimaginative mind, what kind of game of pursuit would ensue? Well, let's wait and see.

Day 4

His inbox:

Wear comfortable shoes. Wear well-worn shoes. Wear shoes that won't skid on a smooth pavement or a waxed floor on a rainy day. Who knows what kind of pavement to expect on the first date? Excessively high heels lack a certain unspoken intimacy. Overly showy colors are risky for someone with plain, unremarkable looks.

Don't enter any store or establishment one is not familiar with. Some people fear transparent floors. Some fear revolving doors that keep spinning, despite the fact that they follow set patterns. These places featuring such unusual designs deflate one's self-confidence.

The above reads like a list of dos and don'ts for a first date. But what I really mean to say is that you are welcome to ask me out, but I hate glassy places glittering with cleanness and uncomfortable places where etiquette is observed to a fault. Not sufficiently pretty or elegant, I prefer not to be invited to a gleaming white or ultramodern place to discuss questions of the soul.

On this gloomy February day, he tried to imagine her dreams. Did he share her yearnings? They would meet. He could imagine the tense, awkward silence at the beginning of the meeting, how her fingers would nervously fidget with the coffee cup, the packets of brown sugar, and the napkin. What would her voice be like? It was easy and assured last time they met, but surely there would be a change this time.

Day 5

His microblog:

I need to write a beginning for the story. How about a fairy tale? Compared to real life stories, a fairy tale is bland tasting, and yet refreshing, like cooled tea re-steeped for a third or a fourth cup. It's easy to add color to a fairy tale, with plenty of stained glass, resplendent and celebratory of the beauty of life! In the finale, a torch, in my hand, would burn it all down. There is no fairy tale, ever, between a man and a woman. There is no fairy tale. That will be the moral of the story. I desperately need an inspiration! For that first sentence!

A reader with a need or a question can discover in the one hundred and forty words that which will guide him for the rest of his life. You often find the deepest meaning in a sentence that appears to be totally meaningless. Her imagination ran wild as she read his microblog. It had been a long time since she last wrote anything, none of which, needless to say, ever got published, although at one time she often pictured her works widely shared. She had no confidence at all in her own talent. She knew what her abilities were. All she wanted was to write a beginning, one that would appeal to him. She would not be writing it for her own sake. What did he want? She wished she were a seasoned writer who could bend her head over her computer and tap out a world unrelated to her life. She wanted to return to her computer. For an imperceptible split second, she felt an obscure urging. It occurred to her that if the beginning she came up with found favor with him, she could then ask for something.

Day 6

Beginning 1:

I'm now going to tell you a fairy tale, a fairy tale about a vagabond. He circles around us, like an early morning mist wrapped about our little room. He walks about and tarries here and there, trying every window, in an attempt to let himself in. I wanted to let him in, my dear. You are not particularly alert. You are fast asleep, all your body hairs slumbering peacefully next to your skin. You are innocent as a baby. No wonder you have been left in this deserted place. The room is snug and so secure. But I feel threatened by the vagabond. I want to go out and tell him a fairy tale, a fairy tale about someone who is fast asleep, a fairy tale about you.

Beginning 2:

(This fairy tale records a real life, our life. It was written the day we first met and instantly fell in love with each other.)

These were words scribbled on the wall of a ladies' restroom in a café. They could already serve as the beginnings of the outline of a story. But I have a strong sense that those words would interest you and you would project us onto that wall, that gaze, cold, conciliatory, into emptiness.

Beginning 3:

A woman is bent on becoming a writer. To

find inspiration she married an author. The author told her that inspiration would cost her. Every time they made love, he would take something from her body. She gave her consent and they made love once a year. After ten years of this, her body exhibited all kinds of freakish deformities, an ear missing, a breast flattened, and other such conspicuous deficiencies. She did produce ten books, which are in libraries now. At the end of the story she killed him, or according to another version, he committed suicide in her arms because he had fallen in love with her. After that all her deformities disappeared and she couldn't stop writing because she never ran short of inspiration, but there were no more men in her life.

She told him this story the first time they made love, for reasons.

Beginning 4:

In the beginning they wanted only one room. A closed space held an irresistible attraction. It would be a quiet space where she could enjoy a good sleep unencumbered by a husband, where she could do as she pleased.

But the story didn't turn out that way. At the

start of the story he wished to torment her. Who do you think you are, he said, you already possess all that you can possess, but you want still more. You want a rare phrase, a phrase that lives only if unspoken. He asked her how she came to know that phrase. She replied that she found it in the eyes of a troubadour. The troubadour told her with his eyes and his body: this phrase lives in a mountain tarn covered by water lilies. It blooms only once in its life span. The moment it comes into bloom, the lake surface glitters with a million golden and silvery light rays that sing. Then the light fades like a spent candle and the phrase sinks back to the bottom of the lake.

He interrupted her, pushing her into the kitchen and assigned her various household chores. You think you are smart, he reprimanded her, how come you can't do anything right? Yes, right under his nose she broke a dish, left the soup to boil over, douse the flames on the stove, and forgot to turn on the exhaust fan, causing the smoke to blow into the room. In short, you are good for nothing except lying on your back, moaning and opening your legs, like all women. You are beyond help.

And tears rolled down her cheeks. Fairy tales are a

wasteland after all. It is time to go home, she thought.

Day 7

Her inbox:

Beginning 1: a quiet voyeur. Beginning 2: flawed beauty. Beginning 3: hard to describe in words, but smacks of an impudent wickedness. Beginning 4: it's as it should be, I think. Yes, absolutely. There is a precarious danger, like a panting body, a body that pants but does not impart a sense of security. I'm glad you wrote these for me (you had always seemed tame to me). I'd like to know something more. I know nothing about you. Your scenario ... Beginning 4, triggered in me a sudden urge to express myself. I sometimes feel that it is foolish to express oneself and writing it down is even sillier. Sometimes I am weak (and I may need your strength). I seem to suddenly and deeply feel the presence of another soul.

By the way, are you a good girl ...?

He did like Beginning 4. He even spent a moment picturing her in the kitchen, perhaps with a scarf tied around her head. Maybe an apron is in order, and a pair of slippers. She'd be surrounded by an army of pots and pans and other cooking paraphernalia. The walls would be rigged with hidden cameras. They are his eyes, peering down benignly. That evening he cooked a stew of pork ribs, tomatoes, winter bamboo shoots, and potatoes. Here was how he conceived of the story:

Since the heroine in the story wished to possess that phrase, the man gave it to her, on the condition that she had to accept it, regardless of what that phrase would grow into, even if it developed into a monster that would devour her. That phrase would start as a little cherub, surrounded by a halo, but would grow bigger and darker, forever demanding more and more with an outstretched hand. Much later its face would become so hideous that she would take fright and cry with such an utter abandonment that the most elegant lady would look like a fisherman's wife. Oh, women's fear of love. All women take fright when faced with true love.

A dark, horror story seemingly meant to taunt her?

But he was unprepared for her response:

"That woman will impart great strength to that phrase. Therefore, it will triumph in the end, overcoming all odds, and the monster will turn into a prince (whether he is handsome is immaterial, he suits her perfectly). The phrase will once again sink to the bottom of the lake, but that's no great loss because with the happy grand finale, there is no longer a need for the phrase, which can safely retire."

The response was distasteful to him. Happy endings represent for him one of the hallmarks of bad taste. How much does literature have to do with her? Could it be a foolish illusion? Among the many things he learned from his first woman was how far a woman would go in order to get her man. So was it a case of a good girl attempting to snare him? Eventually love disappeared, leaving only a residual habit. The woman became hysterical, but at least she married well. In his adult life, he has never felt a need to be responsible in affairs of the heart. Whoever swears fealty to love behaves like those fools who scale mountain peaks only to find they have to come sliding down. That's what men and women do, but it is not what he wants.

Day 8

Lying in his white bed—white quilt cover, white

pillow cases, and white sheets—she wondered if there was a thick coat of dust under the bed. Then she wondered why she would wonder about such things. The room did not excite her curiosity. It was he that she was interested in after all. Only a few minutes ago she was pacing about fully clothed in the room, doing it in order to appear to feel at home. She moved about very carefully on the wooden floor. This was his place. She could sit, pick up a book, or lie on the couch, but doing any of that in this place would appear unnatural. She stood by the window for a moment, but found it chilly. Her gaze fell on an earth green potato that had sprouted on a bookshelf. In a setting like this, you lose your glow and freshness like over washed old underwear, but you gain an appearance of depth and sophistication. It set her to thinking about her own place. The first thing that came to mind was her glassy bathroom, in which she toasted herself first thing in the morning under the heat lamp enveloped by hot steam. Making love leads to a sense of emptiness, taking a bath leads to lovemaking, and therefore to emptiness. Why did she linger so long under the shower? He was waiting for her to come into his bed, and she would do so. Then he took her into his arms. The craving, the need began to generate them and proved so irresistible.

But in the act of kissing, she suddenly wondered who this person was, and who she was, but then it didn't seem to really matter. The fact is both of them felt there was something there and a ripple began to propagate through the air. There was no other alternative. Why would simple words like kissing, penetration, and pumping have anything to do with love? She was suddenly moved to compare her expectant, palpitating heart to the creaking of that not so spacious bed, which took up a quarter of the room's space. The small room, less than thirty square meters, had a life of its own, she thought. It witnessed the beginning of one story after another, unconcerned about their ending. Their story had only just begun.

His inbox:

Making love to you was really enjoyable. I found you had very long arms, firm and hard. Crooked behind my back, they reached across my body to hold me. I could feel myself trembling. I caught it from you. The entering was long and slow, it filled me completely. I pressed my face into the pillow, to stop myself from screaming and from thrashing about. It was a fleeting moment of release that one could die for.

Your rhythm quickened, overwhelming me with wave upon wave of assault. That warm, moist, lightless passage was invaded repeatedly by you. Occasional blankness blacked out my mind. I wanted you, wanted that which was tipped with the tenuous light of a firefly to illuminate my inside with every penetration, until my whole being emitted a faint glow. This glow of shameless illicit love would give me a new gloss of attractiveness.

Then there was the climb down from the climax, which was to be accomplished by me alone.

I have a fear that from now on I will never be able get you out of my heart and mind.

Day 9

His relay story 1:

She didn't really know what to do once out of that room reeking of smoke and liquor. In a corner of her heart, an innocent little shadow, clueless about impending harm, still slumbered under a jumble of quilts. She was, she thought, an ordinary person who thought herself smart enough, a reckless interloper who barged into a life she had no claim to. But the story had only just begun. He was after all decent enough and he made her stay.

Let's see what else we can do in this room besides making love, he suggested. She nodded. The truth was that she needed only to be held in his arms. She was not good at using her imagination. But she believed she could manage. It's hard sometimes to feel sympathy for optimists.

He: Come over here. Let's sit on the sofa, close our eyes, and imagine this setting.

She: It's a huge house, surrounded by dense woods and flowers.

He: I'd rather be in the dark. Don't forget, dear, that it is already night.

She: All right, let there be moonlight flooding the room. Bathed in the faint, golden light, you give a sense of quiet and serenity.

He: You boldly approach me, and the room echoes with the sound of rustling clothes.

She: The floor starts to creak.

He: You are so much shorter than I am that

even when you stand on tiptoe you still cannot reach my height.

She: But I can still feel your warmth.

He: (slightly impatiently) Then the two of them did everything that they were supposed to do.... All right, as a token of gratitude for your company tonight, I am going to offer you a gift. I'll let you pick it for yourself. You can choose a pair of handcuffs made from soft lambskin, adorned with little bells, which will jingle when you try to struggle off the handcuffs tying you to the bed post, or you can choose a clear hourglass containing not sand, but tiny petals, every one of which glitters like crystal. With the hourglass, we can time our lovemaking. If you cause a premature ending of the act, before all the petals sink to the bottom, you will be punished. The last choice is a key, which may fit the keyhole of the entry door of my place now, but may no longer do so tomorrow.

She: (after a moment of hesitation) I wish to have the key.

He: I knew it! You are a person with little sexual curiosity!

She: But curiosity can kill the cat ... I still want the key.

He: All right, now, you must leave this room. Take a ten to fifteen-minute walk, then come back here, take out your key and see what you can open with it. I actually own all three floors of this building. There are many little rooms. Which door will open for you? Remember that when you come back here, the building will be pitch dark, as dark as the bowels of the earth. There will be no moonlight. There will only be a heaviness and closeness in the air.

Day 10

Her relay story 2:

She gazed at the building before glancing at the side road that she had just taken. It was a road like any other, with no twists and turns, and it was illuminated by a street lamp as it turned in from the main road. Can she find him again, she wondered. She would find her way back to the building somehow. So she decided to walk on, and find out what the key might bring to her. The decision had required courage. It was dark, the kind of darkness that obscured her head, shoulders, and her small frame. Would that key produce some faint light? It didn't. The key had lost its entire luster in the darkness.

Remember the labyrinth rules, the right-hand rule. Always keep her hand on the right-hand wall. The walls were probably covered by dust, and maybe some cobwebs. Sometimes the wall felt like glass, cold and brittle. Sometimes her hand seemed to come in contact with something soft, like velvet. As she groped in the darkness, feeling the wall with her hand, Maeterlinck's words popped into her mind: no sooner do we speak than ... the divine gates are closing, and when we hold our peace, the gates reopen. If you close your eyes in an already dark space, it's not dissimilar to a form of meditation in which your whole exterior being is quiet as the silence in the depths of the ocean, and you wait patiently for a flicker of light to issue from your soul. Her heart palpitated. When will the adventure end?

She tried her key in the lock of the first door she came to in the darkness. The key turned and the door lock opened. She was greeted by a uniform blackness, but there was a smell of blood.

She tried her key in the lock of the second door

she came to in the darkness. The key turned and the door lock opened. She was greeted by a uniform blackness, but there was a smell of green grass.

She tried her key in the lock of the third door she came to in the darkness. The key turned and the door lock opened. She was greeted by a uniform blackness, but there was a smell of a swimming pool.

She made her way to the second floor, then the third floor.

She found that the key opened all of the doors. With the opening of each door, the distinct smell held in by that door would rush out to envelop her. She didn't know what she was supposed to do next. So she decided to sit down, right there, on the staircase.

All was quiet. She kept her eyes opened wide out of habit. Suddenly she had the sensation that long thin strands of slender hair, like algae, softly brushed past her face. People seemed to pass before her, the hems of a succession of swaying skirts, trembling slightly, skimmed over the tops of her shoes. Strangely enough, she was not frightened. She seemed to see faces turned to look back at her. Those were beautiful faces, each with its distinct expression, some calm, some angry, some sad, some on the verge of saying something, and some smiling. Those faces were woven into an endless silk shawl that wrapped around her. She could not help heaving a long sigh, the exhalation created such a disturbance that those women's faces vanished.

How did these women enter this building? And how long had they roamed these premises?

Day 11

Her inbox:

The imprisoned.

You have a marvelous imagination. Let this relay of our imaginations continue ad infinitum.

Are you trying to find out the influence of past lovers, my dear? That would be my guess.

True, when you have lived thirty-five years, how can your sentimental journey have been as free of bumpy patches as a plain? Only, the imagery of women's faces was, if I may say so, a bit too direct. If it was up to me, I would probably choose roads, valleys and such, or why not just use the analogy of a journey that takes one through dense forests, across grassy meadows, and sometimes on a road of beaten earth for farm machinery across country where not a spot of green can be sighted for miles around.

Oh, by the way, why were those rooms uniformly black? It wouldn't hurt if they were to have a variety of colors. I have an eye for colors. I can, for example, distinguish nuances of white, lime white, ghost white, eggshell, off white, snow, cream.... Maybe women are more sensitive to smells? After all, their usual place is the kitchen.

As for those women I once loved, they are, when I recall them, like the fast receding trees passed by a car, moving out of sight in a flash. I know I love only you now.

He couldn't bring himself to tell her that the act of recalling the past is like negotiating a muddy mountain road on a rainy day without a raincoat, a hat, or high boots. You keep slipping on a road that is wet and squishy, with fallen leaves that have rotted and turned black. Dampness and gloominess get him down. Why do women think a person unwilling to look back is necessarily cold-blooded? His past lovers A, B, C, D, and E, without exception, faulted him for it. They said the way he turned his back on the past sent a chill through their hearts. He, on the other hand, didn't find anything wrong with it. This way everybody bails out quickly, and starts with a clean slate, returning to single status and waiting to be loved again. But he still managed to land in a pile of rotten hay. He remembered the woman whom he had broken up with a month before. At the moment of final farewell, she turned her face toward him, and what a dazed look it was! That perfectly proportioned body that had so enchanted him and on which he had wanted to notch the days and months and years they spent together with his kisses, those tiny patches constituted by tiny red, almost brownish dots. He had thought that even when that body became disfigured by flab his hands would still linger over it, not out of pity, but lovingly. Her last desperate effort at salvaging their relationship filled him with guilt. The expressions, not the faces, of those women are firmly lodged in his memory, the earliest dating back twenty years.

The look in their eyes, invariably sad at the moment of parting, has been sapping his heart for all these years, so much so that he can't bear to look at himself. His heart was a dying flower in steady decay.

Day 12

His inbox:

I am trying to picture the forests you've penetrated. What will those women enable me to see? They remain in the shadow. I want to watch them, unhurried and calmly.

Day 13

His relay story 3:

She felt a sting on her neck. It was the stem of a rose, the leaves green and the petals tipped with drops of water. It started to emit a faint glow in the dark. She thought she heard the rose say to her: Just stay here and wait, dear. I will bring him to you.

But that was not what she had in mind. She grabbed the rose, which flashed a harsh glint at her, as if frightened. The stem bristled with spikes and her fingers bled. But at least she could see better now. It was an eerie darkness and the space was closed in on all sides. She decided to start with the first door on her right. She walked in. Holding the rose out, she could barely make out that the room was empty. It had a lunette of a window, with a naked Barbie doll on the sill. In the second room she saw a brown desk commonly found in a classroom, with words carved into the top. In the third room she found a necklace and a towel, an old-fashioned one-piece dress and a hat. The fourth room had a bed, actually a small spring cot covered by a bed sheet. When she patted on the bed, a cloud of dust rose up, frightening the rose and causing it to snap back. The white sheet had a faded red smudge on it. After finishing her tour of the third floor, she descended the wooden spiral staircase to the second floor, where she made a major discovery in the second room on the left: a small mirror and a large photo. The face in the photo possessed a pair of big, protruding eyes, seemingly glaring at her. But these paled in comparison with what she found on the first floor, where every room contained a life-size doll that sat in a reclining or supine position on the dust-covered bed sheet. They had long hair that appeared from the abundant dust in the room. All of them surveyed her with their big, beautiful eyes. She slammed the last door shut. Let those dolls go back to the darkness.

Day 14

Her relay story 4:

A shrill voice came through the wall, speaking a word at a time: What. Are. You. Looking. For? Do. You. Know. Where. To. Look?

She replied: I had thought there must be an empty room, but in every room, I found something not belonging to me. So, I don't know where to go from here. Maybe it's time for me to leave?

If. You. Leave. Now. You. May. Never. Have. Another. Chance. To. Come. Back. In. Did she detect a threat in that voice?

But don't you find it a little cruel to leave me in the dark?

What's. In. Those. Rooms. Deserves. To. Be. Left. In. Peace.

What about me?

Since. He. Let. You. In. He. Has. Given. You. Permission. To. Find. Out. But. You. Stand. Between.

Him. And. Them.

During a pause between words, four panes of glass rose slowly from the floor, sealing her off from the rooms, the things in them and from an abundance of dark matter. The glass was so cold that a coat of frost instantly formed on the rose's petals.

Day 15

Her inbox:

What made you come up with the idea of the glass house? Did you want to carve out a small, icy space in which to conduct a dialogue exclusively with yourself? This is not the most felicitous way to communicate. It would be different for the little princess sealed in a glass coffin. But we absolutely don't want a story of princesses and princes, right, my dear? Why do you want to enclose this woman in a shining glass structure? The imagery is very Gothic, but ...

His inbox:

Maybe it's my mediocre talent, but when I wrote

it I had no clear idea what it meant. At the time of writing it, my heart was a dead moon. Maybe I associated that with the coldness of glass? I know you would think it could do with some rewriting. But if that building is likened to the heart of a man, say, your heart, do you think it will be full of tenderness and light in there? You will sometimes be rough with a woman intruder, will you not? Surely, you wouldn't want her to come and go as she pleases....

Day 16

His relay story 5:

She knew she should take a deep breath and deal calmly with the four walls that had sprung up out of nowhere, but the anger was there, an anger that started out as a constant buzz in her ears and she was agonized by this sensation akin to tinnitus. It was made worse by the frustrating sense of having been abandoned, forgotten or mocked by him. The anger was finally borne along the trickle of blood still oozing from the tip of her finger to taint the rose. And a small ball of flame whooshed out of the center of the flower.

Day 17

That afternoon they had afternoon tea together. She wore a tight black skirt, a motorcycle leather jacket and canvas shoes. He sported his usual gray woolen sweater, over a checkered shirt. Protestations about the fear of gaining weight notwithstanding, she finished the whole slice of tea-flavored chestnut cake all by herself. He was the picture of gentlemanly solicitude, and kept filling her cup from a glass teapot. They were sitting on the balcony of a café converted from an old building, where they commanded a view of the balcony of the well-appointed café across the street. Beyond lay an amalgam of indistinguishable rooftops, their dreary colors making them appear hazy even on a clear afternoon like this. She was speaking, mostly about some mundane matters, such as her daily routine, when she left for and return from work, her favorite shopping spots, the need to make allowance for hourly household workers, and her general weariness with life. These words, spoken at this particular moment, reminded him of scenes from Eric Rohmer's film *Love in the Afternoon*. Although he was not wearing a turtleneck, the cardigan zipped all the way to his Adam's apple could equally wrap him in solid, gray solitude. He was made to feel the unreality of his own desires. And this was the most interesting moment, when they were beginning to develop an attachment with each other, and yet at any moment, could leave the other in the lurch. The idea came and went in a flash, causing him to wonder whether he loved with his brain or his heart. Obviously, he was guided by rational thinking. Looking at her face, he thought of his ex-girlfriends. There were not many. He could count them on the fingers of his two hands. There were no set criteria, but they were all the best in their category. He would describe himself as a cage that went in search of a bird, as Franz Kafka wrote in his Notebook. This was actually the simplest way, to be dictated purely by one's own feeling and not to be tailored to the other's needs. "You see, my dear," he would say to them, "I've now given all of me to you, body and soul and heart." Did they really think they could hold him in the palm of their hand?

Going over in his mind those women to whom he had taken a particular fancy, he found that he hit it off with most of them pretty quickly. A couple of them took some wooing, and none offered themselves up to him of their own accord. They were no paragons of beauty and none of them seriously eclipsed the others in his heart and mind. One of them, a childhood playmate, not only dared to imagine copulating with him in the outdoors on a mountain, but actually acted on her imagination, which humanized her stern, awe-inspiring, authoritarian exterior. This woman, who is now a high executive in a foreign corporation, reserved her friendly smiles exclusively for him. Another woman of his had a curvaceous body that fascinated him. Her fantasies about members of her own sex aroused and hardened him. He had high esteem for a pensive ex-lover who was forever reflecting on the chance and necessity of innocence and levity. The woman before his eyes looked somewhat vulnerable. Fortunately, in her profession as an editor she could keep herself safely out of the public eye. His thought turned to himself. He was forever on the cusp of producing a good work (he had meant to use the expression "great work"). Obviously, the work was yet to be written and he therefore felt the solitude of the desert, which he tried to assuage with hard liquor, as a troubadour would do.

Maybe his acquaintance with her had potential significance? After all, she was bold enough to propose alternative beginnings for the story. She was now talking about her "personality that's somewhat at odds with the norm," meaning in short she believed in physical sciences without for that reason believing any the less in geomancy and feng shui. She consulted a practitioner of traditional Chinese medicine once a week, and she was fascinated by the principles of Western medicine, which treats symptoms and specific ailments. She was a believer in astrology and the attribution of particular traits to people of different blood types, and an enthusiastic participant in experiments of divination with the help of a dish or a pen (none of those experiments succeeded in establishing communication with any spirit). Wait, he interrupted her, if you were to really hear the voice of a soul or spirit, whose soul would you like to converse with? After a long silence during which her face assumed a dreamy expression, she replied that she wanted to be able to meet with her grandmother, who died of pancreatic cancer, adding quickly that the grandmother promised seven ounces of gold jewelry to mother but the small case containing the jewelry mysteriously disappeared from the big chest of drawers in which it was kept after the death of the old lady. Her answer smacked too much of realism to be useful for judging her talent and creativity. That was really unfair to my mother, she stressed again.

They became almost simultaneously aware of a shaft of soft light that had fallen on the table and there was a sudden silence.

Day 18

Her relay story 6:

Was the rose possessed?

Was the rose possessed, possessed?

Indeed it was. That glowing anger of the rose pierced the disgusting, oppressive glass walls. That voice from the darkness outside these walls became shrill, as if burned by the fiery ball of anger.

You. Will. Be. Trapped. Here. Forever.

Here. You. Can. Float. And. Drift. About. All. You. Like.

But. You'll. Lose. All. Your. Freedom!

But the rose ignored the warning and flew out from between her fingers, lighting up the little glassed-in space. As it dashed its puny head against the glass, it made a dull, hollow sound.

A cloud of air bubbles started slowly to form outside the glass cubicle. At the sight of those bubbles flying in their individual grotesque manners, she felt a strange painful tightening in her chest, as if she had just been pierced by some gray, gloomy worry. She impulsively tapped on the glass pane, hoping to frighten the bubbles away. Soon another swarm of bubbles surrounded the glass booth. This new raid was worse than the previous assault. Why did those painful memories flash before her eyes once again? She felt the need to tap with more force on the glass. But the third wave of little bubbles brought her a pleasant surprise. They were such a beautiful, graceful lot flying about her glass cage that she couldn't resist an urge to stretch out her hand to touch them. They emanated a sweet scent, in which she could discern the perfumes of rose, jasmine, ginger lily, lavender. Those perfumes, associated since time immemorial with love, had once generously added flavor to her humdrum, insipid life. No life belongs solely to oneself. The web was spun, ready for its prey, and when someone appeared, all ambition evaporated. There was a softening, followed by trembling.

But the most graceful dance would eventually come to an end. Those beautiful little bubbles played a cruel prank on her before leaving. They rubbed themselves against the glass until they all burst in a most unsightly manner, leaving behind a darkish liquid that slid down along the glass until it dried, creating an ink wash effect. The rose lit up, overdoing it a little. As she looked at the black streaks on the glass, she was momentarily visited by a vision of certain afternoons. She wondered if the end of a relationship always happened in the afternoons. There is a certain quiet and restrained quality to the afternoon air, unlike in the night, which is associated with fire and emotions tend to be volatile then, perhaps causing one to violently grab the other? In the white diffused afternoon sunlight, the two sat in a dark corner in a black silence. The black with an ulterior motive disappeared into the white.

Day 19

Her microblog:

A seminar out of town. Three days. A rare opportunity. It was our first trip out of town together. The destination was a city by the sea. The topic discussed was "In Search of Doubt and Despair in Literature." The second day was spent in an outing to the shore. The view was magnificent. There were large crowds of tourists. The souvenirs were of inferior quality and hideous. Mass-produced "craft" articles could readily be found at the market stalls around the City God Temple of Shanghai. It was not until late night that the long yearning was finally fulfilled for a short moment.

The room was pleasant. After a thorough inspection of the room, she telephoned him. His voice felt somewhat sluggish and thick. But she was her usual self. She examined her underwear, her skin and the angle of the lighting. These were tiny details easily missed by the other but they had to be attended to. It was a good way to enchant a man without his noticing it. She had her unique experience in exerting subtle, imperceptible influences.

But he was not thinking about her at this moment. There were at the seminar other women editors who were very pretty, one of whom was considered a beauty by several male participants. As for her, while her facial features were not bad, her body left much to be desired. For one thing, she was not fleshed out adequately and her buttocks appeared to be bloated from sitting too long at her desk. What turned him off most was the aggressive manner in which she made her interventions at the meetings and the vague generalities she spouted. "It seems to me the important thing in literature is not doubt and despair, but honest intellectual exchange." She struck him as smug and self-important. She was lucky to have that literary magazine as her protective talisman. The beauty, on the other hand, sat unobtrusively in a far corner of the conference room, all dressed in black, which accentuated her fair complexion. He had a strong wish to explore together with that beauty the intriguing mysteries of "doubt and despair," a conversation he thought he was well-prepared for given his erudition, but her ceaseless text messages distracted him from exploring the divine gate of that beauty. Too bad, he might as well spend all his energy on the bed sheets.

His microblog:

I hate seminars. What is accurate and to the point is often boring, and it's the ambiguous half-knowledge that is in vogue. Sometimes a critic's pride of his/her life turns on only one keyword. The quintessential seminar melds elegant speech with poorly hidden passion—that is the secret desire of every seminar goer.

Day 20

His relay story 7:

Outside the four glass walls, the voice in the dark intoned again:

Rebuild. Rebuild your own life. Rename it. The two of you together, make sure you understand what affection means to you.

With those words the cold glass walls disappeared and light sprang up. It was the light from the ceiling fixture.

Day 21

Her relay story 8:

She stood in the hallway, not knowing what to do next. In the beginning there was nothing but sweetness in her heart, because she had surrendered herself to the other and there was joy in that submission. She was used to a life regimented like clockwork. Every hour on the hour, the clock would strike. He must think her quite boring and uninteresting, otherwise he wouldn't have ended the game prematurely.

Yes, she was a married woman, destined for better or for worse to live out her life with a single man. Thinking of her husband, she was suddenly struck by how important he was for her. Life is full of possibilities, she thought, and she really shouldn't overindulge her curiosity. Yes, on the whole, the routine changed little: choosing clothes, trying different hair styles, turning the perfumed bath oil scent of her body into the peculiar sweaty smell of post-coitus.

But she could feel the metallic key in her palm.

It suddenly occurred to her that perhaps he imagined her to be a tightly wrapped head of cabbage that invited his probing, teasing and his attempt to fluster her.

Undecided, she twirled the key between her fingertips. Then she attached the key to her own key ring. At least for tonight, she decided to ignore his existence.

Day 22

His inbox:

I'm not particularly pleased with my latest relay story. I had meant it to be a romantic story. Of course, I have never been the apple of anybody's eye. When I was a child, my ambition was to become a novelist. I also dreamed of becoming a poet. I am now neither a novelist nor a poet, but an ordinary editor tending to the needs of some ordinary novelists. Some of them are younger than I, some older, some meek and genial, others wayward and unreasonable. Did a stirring not creep into my heart?

Inspired by a surge of love, I had thought this novel would be truly vibrant and imaginative, growing exuberantly like rank weeds. But it seems now to have lost its ability to dance through the air.

Her inbox:

You will be a good writer. It's not too late to begin a career change now. I rather think your relay story was fine. Love is a cramped little space that has room for a big bed but not for a big imagination.

Day 23

His relay story 9:

But she kept waiting. Her patience paid off. She heard footsteps and he took her into his arms from behind. What followed was quite simple. Lovemaking. Making love is truly a quick way to reconciliation. Undressing. Penetration with curiosity. Tidal waves. He had superb control of his unique gyrating technique, maintained a well-practiced steady tempo punctuated by thrusts of emphasis, followed by abandon and wild movement ending in the emptying of the fluid of desire.

They gazed at each other, across the crumpled quilts. A faint flush suffused her cheeks that seemed to be the result of all the thrusting. She didn't look her usual self. Now her whole being seemed to have been soaked through and had turned transparent like a jellyfish. They embraced with the quilts between them.

He resorted to his imagination when writing this part. He let his mind wander to that pretty editor at the seminar, and the little wings in his groin twitched at the thought. He imagined that woman to be draped in layers of black crepe, which rustled as she walked, her fingers pressing upon her clavicles. That's where the crepe began, and also where it ended. She had a sweet smile but her eyes were sad. This near perfect imagination worked. He believed he could continue to comfort the other woman with his writing, without her discovering the real prototype for the story.

Day 24

She was quite disappointed by how the story relays had evolved. For one thing, the novel was turning out to be unexciting. Then there was the fact that a fond hope of hers which she had kept to herself had been dashed: she had imagined the two of them would sit side by side, and, as the story unfolded, would together build and share. This hope appeared now to be unrealistic, for he had explicitly told her that if he were to reveal it beforehand, he would lose the sense of written narrative.

Maybe relay story telling is only a written narrative, and it's impossible to foresee the ending. Perhaps the ending comes with the end of their relationship?

Her relay story 10:

When she left his apartment, she could see the moon in the sky. But on the way home the weather turned unpleasant. Thick, dark clouds gathered and seemed to weigh on her head. The moon disappeared, and her belly swelled. This usually happened only when she had her periods. She put her hand on her belly and found a round, awkward protrusion there, which was still slowly growing. Something seemed to be floating inside. As she got out of the cab and made her way toward her building, she looked three months pregnant.

Her house was bright and spotless, as if readied for any surprise inspection of its sanitary condition. Her husband was not yet home. She drew the curtains and turned on all the lights. In the bathroom she undressed and found there was indeed a change in her lower belly. It had the opaqueness and translucence of frosted glass. If this was a punishment for her infidelity, it was an uncanny and flawless one.

She imagined a knife drawn across her belly. What would be expelled from there?

Water to cleanse them? Bodywash? Gel-like young life formed by millions of sperms? The moon in the sky? His or her solitude? Or, would it be all those lies? Maybe none of the above, but some icy cold, wet and sticky, stinking stuff anyone could easily imagine. It was at this moment of her reverie that the huge, terribly crumpled bed came into her mind once again and the belly, where the evidence of infidelity is hidden. What if a woman carried on illicit affairs with more than one person? Would there be bellies in conflict and occupying opposing camps? What if the illicit affairs multiplied? Bellies would swell up in competition and the torso would gingerly pick its way among them. Only true love that survived to the finish would get to evolve into her real self, but why is it that one instinctively associates water with femininity?

Day 25

Her inbox:

I happen to have portrayed in a novel of mine a pseudo feminist, who relished talking about body fluids. Perhaps it's because women like to imagine themselves hosts to a variety of body fluids? Body fluids represent a self-expression, as well as self-tolerance. Women are enthusiastic about soaking in baths. They are fascinated by the thought of being submerged in water. It can even be said that the rippling water surrounding a woman represents all desires. But for her body fluids, a woman would wilt and fade. Body fluids are women's vernal love. They should radiate a light of verdant life. Is that why women are meek and pliable like the young sprigs of spring?

Day 26

His relay story 11:

What's in here? Her husband lay down beside her, his briefcase standing between their legs. He flipped her nightgown to discover that almost translucent belly. There seemed to be something inside, but he couldn't make out clearly what it was. Muttering indistinct words under his breath, he slid his finger across her belly futilely. Then he saw a man's face slowly detach itself from among the shadows flickering on the belly. Who is this? He brought his face closer. All of a sudden the man's face was catapulted onto the tip of his nose, causing him to flinch as if from an electric shock. He sat up in a huff. Who is this?

They stared at each other.

Sorry ...

Sorry for what?

I ... and someone ... I don't know ... how it got that way down there....

The husband fell silent. He bowed his head, and took out a cigarette. He drew deeply at it and lit one after another, as if he depended on this to come to an understanding of what he was seeing. He cast an occasional glance at her, in a depressed mood. The ash fell from the cigarette. And fell. The almost milky white belly kept rising imperceptibly. She tried unsuccessfully to suppress it in silence.

Day 27

Lunch was served in bed. He had made a pot of chicken soup, in which were added vegetables and shreds of bean curd sheets.

Do you wish me to stay the night? She asked.

I think it's better that you go home tonight ... we can have supper together and go out for a movie. What do you think?

You don't want me to stay?

...

No, I shouldn't have come here in the first place, taking a taxi and offering myself up like this....

That's nonsense.

She got off the bed. He did the same and watched her make the bed.

I wanted you to be happy ... I wanted you to stay.

Happy?

Aren't you happy?

She flashed a smile at him. It's not a good idea for a woman to allow herself to be so easily aroused. Look at what happened to me.

What happened to you?

Her hand deftly tucked the corners of the bed sheet under the mattress. I have a feeling that you have cooled toward me. I can see it from the way you wrote the relay stories. But I can stand a bit more coolness from you. I think I will not behave this way again in the future.

Her microblog:

There was a stone fireplace in the room. The carvings were not of the finest quality, but the venetian blinds were interesting. The wardrobes were not locked, and clothes could be seen hanging inside. There was an abundance of books, dining utensils sat on the low table in front of the sofa, a notebook computer on the desk, a batik cloth with blue floral patterns, a floor lamp, a desk lamp and a home audio system. Standing in the room amidst all that, I felt so inferior, so stupid.

Something is ebbing.

His microblog:

Love is a constantly falling, colorless, odorless gas. It comes quietly and gradually swallows up everything. In the beginning, the air shimmers with a bright light, but eventually the luster becomes monotonous and dull. The gas closes in on you, fills your entire being and weighs you down until everything becomes a blur.

He couldn't pinpoint the reason. He had thought that since they had been thrown together, maybe it was possible to stay together for a while longer. But it turned out otherwise. He just felt tired. He had made a generous decision to give her a year, but now it seemed that even half a year was more than sufficient.

Day 28

Her relay story 12:

That night, her husband slept in the living room and she stayed in the bedroom. The room, normally pitch dark if the light was not turned on, was now illuminated by a soft glow from the opalescent belly. She stared at her moon-like belly and his vaguely visible face on it, feeling lethargic and serene and finally sinking into sleep.

An excruciating pain in her belly awakened her. Her husband was trying to bind her belly with a rope made by stringing together all ribbon-shaped fabrics he could find in the apartment: pink long towels, colorful scarfs, bed sheets shredded into ribbons. Something in her belly seemed to be hiding and dodging, tightly clinging to her inside, one moment protruding from under the taut rope and then slipping away the next.

"I did some research online. The evil desire for illicit love can only be exorcized once and for all by tying the offender tightly with a fabric rope."

Her husband's mouth gave off a damp cold stench of iron. She struggled in an attempt to break free, but something was continuously dripping from her lower body. Her husband muttered, "How many times did you do it with him? You are so wet. It appears I need to use all of these fabrics." The only word that caught her attention was "wet." Clearly all the body fluids that had accumulated in her were now emptying out.

Day 29

Her inbox:

I read your story. I really don't know.... Are you envisioning their breaking up? This unusual description of an "aborted birth" made me mourn the loss. But I absolutely respect your idea. Perhaps it was a faithful description of reality—are you saying she was ending once and for all the illicit affair and decided to go back to her family?

His inbox:

Yes, although everything lasted only a few moments, I hope that I behaved with restraint, be a nice lady, and abstain from greed and clinginess. Imagination helps me attain what I consider the ideal state between man and woman. Perhaps that's what will happen between you and I? I truly would rather give you up in order to return to my place and cherish the memory in my heart.

Her inbox:

No wonder ... between the lines I could read a sense of art imitating life. It seems metaphors are always drawn from observations of real life.

Day 30

His relay story 13:

Her belly having returned to its former flatness, she had no more excuse to continue her confinement in the apartment. At daybreak, she took a shower, got dressed and after telling her husband she was going out. Even with her exposed indiscretions, she could not fail in the matter of good manners. She closed the apartment door and left. She wanted to take a gamble with her fate: she would walk along the street in front of their building and if the first person she ran into was a man, she would go with him; if it was a woman, she would live the life of a single woman; if it was a child, she would go back home and try to salvage her marriage. She found little difference between the three choices as far as she was concerned.

But she did not run into a man, a woman, or even a child.

She came across a dog and a cat, which were running in her direction, chasing and tangling with each other. She was very much surprised at how well the cat and the dog got along with each other.

But what could this suggest?

Perhaps it suggested that you must live your feeling, or that life itself had little meaning; that you should be open to trying anything, because after all, you would eventually crumble into dust without rhyme or reason; perhaps choosing itself was unwise because you did not have the possibility to review all the options.

She chose to stay at a hotel. Two hermetically shut windows in the room insulated the interior from the daytime noises. She looked at the spacious bed covered with a white sheet and thought: this is where I want very much to lie down.

She saw herself again in the bathroom mirror, haggard, with new creases on her face. Apparently the secret had been safely stashed away in the depths of her being.

Day 31

Her inbox:

There was no joy to speak of, nor sadness, just an endless alternation between sleeping and waking. Not choosing may just be the best choice.

Perhaps one day we will write a completely different story. Maybe she did not want to indulge her curiosity from the beginning; maybe she will stay for him; maybe he will leave her for someone else. Whatever her fate, all these scenarios could possibly happen to you and me.

Curiously, once a story is begun, it develops its own dynamics. Is this a mysterious power of the story, or is it dictated by the inevitability of fate?

His inbox:

Forget. Me. The end is finally here.

I would much rather be simply a friend of yours. I prefer a tenuous but enduring relationship. On the road of carnal love, going up is but an illusion. What is real is the narrow trail coming down, returning to quiet solitude.

She She

I have moved three times since I've known her.

My first home was in a residential compound, in a building set way back from the streets. There was a green space in front but not much in the way of plants. I lived with my ex-husband there for a year. After I moved out, the rusty steel door was replaced by a sturdy burglar-resistant one. Inside, however, little had changed, except for some cardiac medications that weren't there before. As I stood there watering the plants he had left in my care, I wondered, with a twinge of guilt, why did I want change?

She was surprised when I informed her over the phone that I had gotten married. I wanted to know why she did not share my joy. She said marriage did not become me. Maybe, much earlier, before any man had appeared in my life, I could have sailed out of the attic of my home and headed straight for a completely different life. But then would I have met and known her?

The first time—I don't remember the exact date and time—I set my eyes on her was on an evening in early winter at a dinner party in a restaurant. At the table, a bunch of middle-aged men, who were strangers to me and whose wealth was superior to mine, were making merry and loud. There was a supercilious young girl sitting opposite her, who vaunted herself not merely as a writer but even more as a beauty. Pretty faces came and went at such gastronomic gatherings like in a game of musical chairs, but that evening I came away with a new-found friend.

I was not attracted to her at first sight. She wore makeup and was dressed in a long violet coat with a simple clean cut that would not easily go out of style (she was still wearing it last winter). Her smiles, her bright voice (to the point of sounding shrill), her entire being evoked the image of a dog-eared fashion magazine cover. Her hair was jet black (she never dyed it). When that girl referred once more to herself as a pretty authoress, she began to fire questions at her. They were scathing questions. I was a silent observer of their cat-and-mouse game. Soon the "pretty authoress" bent her hardened face toward her plate and started eating in silence. She left the table before the restaurant's famous scrumptious chicken casserole was served.

The moment the door slammed shut after the

"pretty authoress," she turned in my direction (she sat a few seats away to my right) and our eyes met. I smiled at her. I'm not sure if she winked at me. Anyway, there was a look of contentment and familiarity on her face, as if we were complicit in the episode. Two total strangers were able to read each other's mind without exchanging a word, although I had not let my dislike of that girl show. We had occasion to play this game again at another time. I continued to play the part of a delicate silent partner in the duet. Verbally provoking a third woman was quite meaningless but it was great fun. I enjoyed this kind of game. It felt thrillingly wicked.

That explains why we hit it off.

We left the party early. We stood at the curb looking at each other. She was half a head taller. I can still hear the clicking of her boots on the pavement. At the time, I was not comfortable with high heels. Young women with literary aspirations in sneakers eventually allow themselves to stoop to the level of the petit-bourgeoisie. In the matter of dress and fashion, I've since followed in her footsteps.

Shortly afterwards I was invited to her dormitory for singles. As we walked past similar little rooms along the corridor, girls inside were watching TV and none of them paid any attention to us. Look around! This is my home, she said, suddenly clearing her throat as if a little embarrassed, although my face gave away nothing. I saw a bed, a TV facing it, a telephone and a fluorescent light. Some magazines and books leaned haphazardly against one wall. From the way she dressed from top (her hair received regular attention from her stylist) to toe (those polished, glittering shoes of various styles often costing a thousand yuan a pair), nobody could have known that she lived in a dormitory like this. She had a weekly appointment for a facial at her beauty salon, but acne just refused to leave her alone and seemed encrusted on her face. As I fiddled around, she got a call. It was a man's voice. If I were forced to stay cooped up in this tiny room I would lose my sanity sooner or later. She was still talking on the phone.

Later that year, on Christmas to be precise, I picked up my marriage certificate. The ID photo showed me wearing a red sweater and contact lenses. My face was turned a fraction to the left and a smile played on my face, a smile celebrating the marriage, but it was a restrained and reserved smile. Where was this man F at that moment? What topographic feature lurked in my marriage that would prove advantageous to him? He was still out of my eyeshot. I waited in my own world, knowing only that the future was unpredictable. Months later F walked into my life and in the short span of a year disappeared from it. He and that big suitcase he lugged, which reminded one of a woman's big swaying bum, walked out of the gate of the residential project and got into a taxi, which turned a corner and disappeared, without leaving any visible trail of exhaust.

It was a quiet moment.

There was another quiet moment like this.

It happened when she, a girlfriend of hers and I were walking on a street in the midday sun. It was not a wide street at all, but it took on a wide openness in my memory because of the glare of the sunlight. She went on about that man: he was tall, already had a paunch and wore glasses. He was all she cared about. For her the world had been reduced to one man. I couldn't care less about that man. But a married man was a novelty to her. She had to grapple with a host of conundrums. She faced one that day. Whenever I open the box of memories, I could still hear her shrill voice going on and on. He was in a car accident, and she wanted to visit him at the hospital, even if she could only see him through a glass partition. She pictured his leg flopped limply on the bed. She imagined him repeating her name in his heart, and having to sit up to sip the soup brought by his wife. The wife was very pretty with short hair like a man. My friend paced back and forth in the street, apparently torn by anguish. I followed behind her, in no hurry to catch up. I may have paused a few times. Her girlfriend was trying all this time to calm her down. All of a sudden she raised her voice to an unwarrantedly high pitch, saying she hated that woman and wished she were dead. What did she do wrong? I retorted. It's you who stole her husband. She glared at me, fuming with anger, and rolled her eyes. I averted my face. I could feel her venomous eyes boring into my back. To stop her from rashly dashing to the hospital, we each held her arms until she gave up, her icy eyes casting a hostile glance at us. I guess every child has at some point glared at people like that. Holding her arm, I found my eyes look past her to fall on a few crude dwellings at the side of the road, their doors open, exposing the exiguous interiors in all their details. I seemed to see that little room of hers, just like a cell in a prison block. She was in that little room, drawing her prince on a white horse with color crayons. In front of those crude one-story dwellings stood a spittoon holding a sunflower plant. On the roofs, a few straggling tufts of weeds grew between the roof tiles. Above them was the sky, a white expanse. I don't remember if clouds covered the sky.

Hate. I heard mother use that word when I was fifteen and have not heard that verb again since then or have heard it only rarely. Hate is a product of love, a rib from love's side. I gently disengaged my arm from hers and told her I loved her. We continued to walk down the street. An utter stillness settled around us, as if something had seized up.

Three other women had been involved with F, two of whom were women writers. They were like female combatants in the field. They had either expressed themselves from a distance or had got involved in close quarters skirmishes. F chose to take the high road with a virgin, and he felt like he was an adolescent again. But then he met me. After my divorce, two different versions of that meeting were in circulation. According to one, I was bed-ridden after an attack of vasospasm and he bought painkillers for me. I was so moved I fell straight into his arms. The other version had me overwhelmed by a sudden surge of lust when I was discussing Sartre with him. The sources of these accounts were acquaintances of mine, editors of newspapers and contributors to magazines. These accounts have faded without a trace now.

I strayed from the high road a long time ago.

Shortly after my first change of residence, she also moved to a place not far from mine. She often asked me to her home to keep her company. We took the elevator from the underground garage, again her high heels clicking on the gloomy floor. I entered the elevator, pressed the button and the elevator ascended slowly. I walked out of the elevator into her world.

She opened the door and placed my sneakers next to a conspicuous pair of men's slippers in the shoe closet she just opened. She offered a pair of slippers for me to change into, but I chose instead to walk on the marble floor in my stockinged feet, which made no sound on the floor. She motioned for me to sit down. She sat straight-backed at first but soon assumed a cross-legged posture and put her clasped hands between her feet. The world seemed to be inhabited only by the two of us sitting opposite each other.

Unable to stand that huge creamy white leather sofa, I crossed the room to the glass door and, leaning against it, looked at the balcony. Beyond it were clusters of small dwellings in the distance. No trees were visible. Even if there were any, I wouldn't be able to name them. Of course, I would recognize the common trees, because they lined the streets of the city. Anyway, this spacious apartment with two bedrooms and a living room was all glass, steel and marble, with not a spot of green, and let in scant sunlight, which might account for the pallor on her face. While her apartment was very different from mine, which was situated in a traditional *shikumen* (stone girded gate) style community of alleys with no shortage of greenery, it was already a big improvement over the dormitory that used to be her home. She once showed me the billets doux she wrote in the dorm and they stirred up memories of the first few mornings of panic after I fell in love for the first time. I prefer the style of letter paper of a bygone era. I remember how the first love letter I wrote felt in my hand. The paper was brand new. I wrote with a fountain pen I selected after painstaking comparisons. I dislike ballpoint pens that often come scented. Scented or not, first loves are always ill-starred.

My mind strayed again. I woke from my reverie when I heard my name called. Apparently she had lost her patience.

She did not offer a tour of the apartment. She didn't want me to see her bedroom and picture their moments of intimacy, I supposed. I once saw her with the man. He struck me as humble and courteous. It was a mask he meticulously maintained. That urbane demeanor so becoming of a scholar must have captured the heart of many women. He was good at making money and enjoyed trifling with the affections of young girls. I understood him, for I would do the same if I were in his shoes. Even after she finally left him, he never said in so many words that they had broken up. I love you, or I don't love you, are hard words to utter and equally hard to explain. Stonewalling builds dramatic tension. As a writer I do sometimes use such techniques in the plot. But in real life I would just turn it off with impatience.

I introduced her to the nanny who worked for me. She had a rotund body wrapped in tight clothes and had small features. When she worked, she bustled about the apartment like a hen, making a great fuss.

In that period we saw each other quite often.

I never let on to her that I disliked her cavalier attitude in restaurants. Waitress! She would yell with a high-pitched voice, clearly articulating each syllable. These clarion notes ringing out from time to time next to my ears often created an instant hush in the restaurant. She would proceed to upbraid the poor girl for poor service. I had an urge to muzzle her, like a veteran hit man screwing a silencer onto his gun, but I sat on my hands. Her eyes spoke of a bitterness that had obviously been festering for a long time, but her confidences did not elicit the expected response. I looked at her with calm eyes and a sober head. You shouldn't think like that. You should stop. Those negative sentences of mine only drew out more emotional outpourings. I stared into my plate with knitted brows, as if the food were something alien.

My analysis and her outpourings followed a familiar pattern. We could go on for hours: I love him very much. No, you will fall in love with others in the future. I have given so much to him. That's why you should immediately stop giving more. It is a bottomless and no amount of affection can fill it. He loves his child. He can't divorce his wife because the kid is too young. If he wants to, he can do it right away. The child knows his parents are miserable together. We must have discussed the question of selfishness and the karma of being a victim or an inflictor of pain. She would phone me despite the lateness of the hour and I would stare at my hands with a frown or start flipping through a magazine as she talked. Once I didn't register a word she was saying. I was riding on top of F holding the handset. At first he still had his eyes fixed on me and we both waited for her to wrap up, but then he gave up with a look of despair. She said she was sorry. Her whining voice was polite. She apologized for having carried on for so long, then she heaved a sigh, a long sigh worthy of Qin Xianglian, that character in the *Dream of the Red Chamber* of long, long ago. It's okay. I spoke with a faraway voice. I never deliberatively and maliciously allow our quickened, heavy breathing to be heard by her, not once.

The first time she mentioned her intention to break up with the man, I felt a great relief. I forget what I did at the moment. I probably did not jump with joy, but I was definitely excited. I gave her a long pep talk before sending her on her way. When she passed me she turned and gave me a smile like a woman soldier embarking on a mission. The erectness of her back, paired with the clicking of her high heels, bespoke courage and resolve. I was sure that I could finally retire from my role as a hotline.

That morning, after boarding the number one subway, I found a spot near a door at the back of the car. I did not tell my ex-husband right away, and we stood there without exchanging a word as the train pulled into and out of several stations. Finally I decided to come out with it. I am going to leave you. After the utterance of these six words, God ordered Moses to stretch out his staff over the Red Sea, and the sea parted between the two of us, and between us and the rest of the riders, revealing narrow passages. I assiduously avoided looking at him, but I could still see his orange T-shirt, this erstwhile security blanket of the color of the sun. Before getting married, he said he was going to take a gamble. Now the waters had flowed back and he had bought an apartment elsewhere and was doing some other things. For the entire summer, from June to September, before the application for the divorce certificate was filed, he only called once, to say I was cruel, and he cried as he said it. He didn't know that outside the window Cupids were making noisy bets on whether there was still any eternal love.

It was at my place that she told me they were back together. Then she proceeded to give a full account, leaving out not the minutest detail. I regarded her as if she were a show. Oh this woman! The pimples on her face suddenly got embarrassed and became flushed one after another in a chain reaction. Why was she unable to wean herself from him? I came to the sad realization that I was powerless to help her. The same scenario had played out time and again for three years now. I detected a set pattern. In those three years, people felt her bitterness before she even arrived or opened her mouth. When she arrived, she would stand in the middle of the room without taking off her coat. Her restless tension filled my little apartment to bursting. She peppered her endless tirades with the word *nuisance!* We had several falling outs but always managed to make up. You look great, her girlfriends would gush. But moments like this were few and far between. In public with the presence of strangers, she always flashed a brilliant smile. She had retained her good looks, a narrow chin, big eyes and all. My poor girl!

Do you know what a nice, kind-hearted woman

his former wife was? She was summarily displaced by his latest woman. The hostility in her words grated on my ears. How can you be sure his present wife is unkind and unworthy of compassion? This was a case of "one word setting off a tidal wave of reaction," if anything was. But I couldn't look away. I held her eyes resolutely instead. A person's eyes don't tell lies. A rabid, desperate little monster lurked in the depths of her eyes. Stop saying that! Have you ever really loved? Have you experienced the pain I am suffering? I knew what she meant by those words. Who hasn't experienced all those things? Pain spares no one, the good, the bad, the base, and the noble-minded alike. In my writing career many a grim life ended voluntarily with a bottle of pills was piously burnished to a fault under my pen.

Tears started streaming down her face, silently and extravagantly, as if those were not her own tears. I often had an urge to hug her, but I never took the step toward, fearing that my awkward outreach would be deftly dodged by her. It's only love! There are a lot of other things to occupy you. No, without him, I can't do anything. I was flummoxed. I was able to write ten thousand words a day because my heart was not romantically entangled. The hot chocolate in front of her was getting cold. Shouldn't you be more optimistic? But I knew there was nothing that should be or must be done a certain way. I nudged her hot chocolate toward her, and she cupped it between her hands but did not drink from it. I always suggested that she order hot chocolate because it would supposedly catalyze some kind of chemical reaction in her hormones to simulate the antidepressant effect of SSRIs (selective serotonin reuptake inhibitors.) She rarely allowed her body to be totally relaxed. You'd never catch her sprawled in a chair. Her arms were often crossed at an acute angle, as if I were not the only person present in the room but there were an unseen other seated opposite her in judgment, before whom she must maintain a haughty demeanor and not to appear to grovel.

But my nanny told me that she was always bringing the man his slippers, taking off or putting on his socks for him and giving him massages. How demeaning! My cheeks burned with shame. Stop! I refuse to listen to any more of this! There was a violent jerk of my mouse. The word "groveling" sprang to mind. I saw my mother do such things for my stepfather. I saw my boyfriend's mother grovel and wag her behind in front of her over-the-hill man friend. Disgusting! I'm sure the two mothers realized this afterward. Yes, disgusting. Just because with the help of that man, my mother was allotted an apartment in a public housing project in which she could have her own hot water bath, she was so flattered and felt so indebted that she gave him a back massage and boiled water to give him a foot bath. When the other man gave the old mother a pair of earrings studded with ruby on her birthday, she asked if it was real. When he nodded, she was so overcome with joy that she didn't know where to kiss him. With her hands on her hips and her back to him she turned her head around and started to wiggle her waist. All this filled me with anger. No, anger was not quite the right word. When I was fifteen, I decided in annoyance and indignation to never put myself in a situation of groveling before and ingratiating myself to a man. Had it been in my power, I would have thrown all those shaming women into the ocean, and would have popped them like bubbles of sea spray. But I swung to the other extreme. When I was alone, I would seek out certain types of novels and disks. I watched those women with beautiful, seemingly immaculate bodies being defiled. The humiliation in their expressions became almost too much to bear, but my eyes were riveted nonetheless. It was not easy to resist the temptation. Once I watched from dawn till night. It almost seemed I was tied and bound to the women in the novels.

The year I lived with F, I chanced upon a girlfriend from high school days in a bar. She was dancing with her face toward me in a far corner. She subsequently called at my home a few times. We sat on the floor. When she hugged me from behind, I sensed a stiffening of my back. We sat rigidly in that posture for a while before her hand dropped to pick up her cigarette. What now? I asked her, without turning my head. Let's go to a hotel, she said.

The ritual of undressing was not much different, but I stayed longer than usual in the bathroom. She had turned off all the lights. I had taken out my contact lenses and everything looked farther away than usual. I couldn't see far. Finally I groped to the side of the bed, which was a twin bed, plain and dull and totally lacking in style. How far could I go in a bed like that?

I didn't notice the date. I should have kept a diary.

I was very sore with all the thumping. That summarized that night. I was sure she didn't use the right technique, but I was not sure what the right way should be. I could feel her smooth belly, as she lay on top of me like a boy. Stupid boy that kept bumping into me with her bony body! I began to caress her with my smaller-than-average hands. My fingers were, as it were, on their way home. They were moving in the right direction, but I couldn't get there. If I could get there, maybe there would be hope for us. I eventually gave up inside of me. This was an important journey and I needed to stay the course, and must reach the destination, but I had given up inside of me. All I knew was there was no alternative to living with a man.

That's how that night went. I tried it a few more times after that, but every time I came away alone and lonely. No marks of any sort were left on the gently massaged skin.

I only went with her once to a foot massage parlor. That proved an unforgettable experience. I had never heard a lustier cry. It was a massage parlor manned by blind staff. We lay on two folding recliners next to each other. She held a magazine in her hands. Two middle-aged blind men perched on low stools at our feet wrapped our feet in white towels. She had always had the demeanor of a young girl, but the pair of kneading hands caused her to wriggle. It tickles! She cried. It tingles! She cried. She started to moan loudly. Her moaning was punctuated with giggles, as if she wanted the blind masseur to stop. She was now transformed into a little woman and the sounds she made were most unbecoming. I noticed heads turned to look at her. I also saw that my masseur turned his face in her direction. She appeared to be on the verge of an orgasm, with her head thrashing and her small white even teeth showing. She did not notice my annoyance.

I don't know if there is a God and if so how long He had been standing there in heaven watching. Maybe He had been there all that time, watching me watching her.

I like to hang out with pretty girls. How old was I when I said that? Eight? Ten? Those girls had a chest as flat as mine, and their hips were no wider than mine. When I was eight I once grabbed a dumpling with meat fillings from my desk mate, a poor bespectacled boy, who put up a valiant fight to defend the dumpling his grandma bought for him. The dumpling, together with the plastic bag, was finally pried loose from his tightly clasped fist. He spat at me angrily. The expectoration landed on my dress. The girl with a pigtail sitting in the row before us pretended to be reading a textbook with her chin on her hand. She knew I grabbed the dumpling for her benefit. During class, the boy pricked me with a pencil. I nearly cried out with pain but stopped myself.

When I was ten I got involved in a melee to help a girl. It was an afternoon probably nobody else would remember. The boys looked mean and menacing, and we retreated to the verge of the sand-filtered drinking cistern. The girl and I stood back to back. Then I fell into the cistern. She pushed her! The boys spoke in unison. Our gym teacher put me in a flatbed tricycle and took me to a doctor, who was kind and courteous. You need some stitches. You don't want to have your face permanently ruined. He had a gentle voice, but I can't recall that kindly face anymore. I received seven stitches. When I told her about it, she brought her face closer to examine my face. It's not very noticeable, she said, that doctor did a good job. The skin over my cheekbone still bears a barely noticeable scar thanks to that girl. I can't clearly recall her face now, nor how she shifted her timid eyes the moment I returned to class. But I do remember her name.

These are such prosaic, unexceptional memories! Just like the man she once loved. After the fireworks comes darkness. After the glamour comes the humdrum.

We went to unimportant dinner engagements together. We shouldn't have taken a taxi to offer ourselves up like that. We were not without means, and we could perfectly well afford our own dinners and enjoy our own company and conversation. Looking back, I wonder why we had put up with all that business of applying makeup and dressing for the occasions. We had dinners with those men several times a week. They were mostly middle-aged. They plied her with liquor while I focused on my food, oblivious to what was going on around me. Men lost interest in me pretty quickly. They talked among themselves. Then someone got to his feet holding his wine cup, his eyes fixed on her. He chuckled as he told the waitress to top up my friend's cup. Those men's nostrils, with hairs they never remembered to trim sticking out, flared wolfishly as if they were trying to catch her scent. She never wore the same perfume for long. The other men sat there, rooting him on by the looks in their faces. If there were other women at the table, they mostly took satisfaction in the misery of others. I remember one combing her fingers through her long hair and coldly smiling. They seemed to be only too glad to see her stagger and finally fall in a heap onto the sofa in the private banquet room and make a public spectacle of herself. She was now flushed with all the liquor she had downed. She laughed uncontrollably, her voice rose to a high pitch and she was slightly out of breath. I seemed to hear many voices calling me by my nickname. Come! Come and get it if you can. The boys lobbed my book bag to each other, with me running and leaping to try to catch it, mostly in vain. After several minutes of these futile attempts I cried uncle, giving breathless cries and laughing, begging them to give back my satchel. The book bag finally landed, spilling the pencil case and its content on the ground. Fortunately, neither she nor I had large bosoms. Big breasts tend to bounce wildly and awkwardly when you cavort like this. For a fleeting moment I felt choked by anger and I wanted to thwack someone. When you beat up a boy, you can kick him in the exact center of his chest. With a girl, you slap her like in the movies. What's the matter, are you okay? I could clearly hear her calling me, and I breathed easy again. Then the clatter of chopsticks and chinaware resumed as I resumed eating, and I was brought back to the reality of the dinner party.

Many were the times when people just saw past

me, as if I were the "Hollow Man." As we got into a taxi together, she said: Those men are disgusting! I couldn't tell if she said it in a tone of indifference or satisfaction. Those dinner parties lasted till F moved to another city and I found a new boyfriend. My rental apartment was now quite far from her place. One room in my apartment served as living room and bedroom. The second room was my study. The apartment had remained vacant for a year before I took it. I repainted the walls in white and green. It was a quick paint job with no thought given to elegance. The paint odor gave me a headache that lasted a full day. I had not had occasion to use the gas stove because there were so many dinner parties. Who are the invitees nowadays? We were young then. These women are young too, possibly younger than we were when we attended those parties. And she got married. She probably was having supper only with her lawful husband, who arrived home at seven or eight in the evening. When he went to work and she found nothing to do at home, how would she pass the time? I could picture her lying in and getting up late, then sitting in front of the TV with her head leaning on one hand. And it was only noon time.

I wonder why I never get bored. I would just turn

on my computer and start typing away. The windows and doors were kept tightly closed and insulated from the noise and din. Two trees stood outside the window. Across the street stood the residential blocks. The air conditioner whirred and amid its rough inhalation and exhalation I indulged in my indescribable little joys. She was at the origin of this long, long journey of indescribable emptiness. One day in June she told me she was getting married. Why don't you write a novel about the two of us? She said. What did she think I could write? She steepled her fingers and opened her eyes wide, trying her best to look innocent. The less than ideal shape of her mouth was only improved when she smiled. She would often pick a tight-fitting flowered skirt made of some synthetic material that exaggerated the bust and accented a narrow waist. I really wished she would stop buying those cheap brands. It maddened me. Why couldn't she give natural fabrics a try, particularly real silk and linen, my favorites? She complained about not earning a decent enough wage. Well, that was a universal complaint. But I kept my opinion to myself. She preferred to present to the world her own natural face, unspoiled by makeup. She struck a pose before me as if ready for a camera shot, knowing that she was perfectly photogenic. It was as if I were possessed by an evil genie that drove me to show her what she refused to see. I fixed her with a derisive look, watching as her face twitched with pain. She flinched, and begged me to spare her the pain, to stop writing: you will ruin my happiness! I continued typing relentlessly, unmoved. After so many years, I finally had her. With her eyes tightly closed, she asked me in a shrill voice to quit doing it. The computer is truly a potent tool. Emitting heat, it acted like a burning hot pair of black plastic handcuffs that was slapped on her wrists to haul her back to me. She didn't know that I had always derived pleasure from torturing ants and flies since I was a child. What about you? You watch from the sidelines as a reader. You stand regarding us without expression, as if we were a show that had been laid on for you but which you find not very interesting. But she didn't want me to continue writing it; she didn't want people to know her story, fearing disruptions in her life. Did she really believe literature was capable of producing any significant impact?

Something passed through my body, sending an involuntary shiver along my spine. I was sure she had cast a curse on me, or at least she was thinking of doing it. When would I lose her?

In her last email to me she wrote: Better not write that stuff. She called the novel "that stuff." No, I said to myself, I won't stand for it. She didn't phone me, because I turned off my cell phone ahead of time. She certainly had the air of someone in a position of power, but I was intrepid and persistent. I would plow ahead with blind resolve. Fortunately she was not vested with the power to muzzle people. If she had lived nearby, who knows but that she would have come sweeping in and plump herself down before my computer desk to inspect my writing, pausing at outrageous passages and rescanning them with her dagger-like eyes.

I consider myself a writer. But was this creative work? I was only typing in a haphazard manner. Creative writing is too large a term, too serious. Only the masters write creatively. My gifts are middling. She had tried all along to comfort me. She said I was a diligent writer. But diligence is never enough. When I am alone and there is nothing I particularly want to purchase online, I would start typing on the keyboard. In the past I would rest only when I had an attack of vasospasm. That kind of dull pain took its time coming and going. I seriously wondered then if I would kick the bucket in my fifties. I almost became an expert in different kinds of pain killers. She always tried to stop me. You can't go on taking these drugs, she would say imperiously. One evening a shot of pain went through my head. I lay down on her sofa and she tiptoed toward me like a kitten. I'll cook you something nice, she offered. She made a "sandwich" of fruit jelly and omelet, which I had a hard time swallowing. Despite the pain I finished off those small pieces of soft slippery fruit jelly. It was a long, agonizing night, but looking back with fresh eyes, I feel deeply touched by the affection she showed me.

Visiting Taobao, the online shopping site, has become my latest obsession. How far gone am I in indulging in the pleasures of this virtual shopping mall? I have already achieved the 4-heart status, that's how far. But given my lean wallet I really shouldn't desire so many things. I've been so engrossed I can no longer do anything else. I've tried to force myself to navigate away from the site, but keywords such as alligator hides, ostrich leather and kidskin keep churning in my brain. They don't leave me alone and I don't know how to choose. I like the colors of animal hides and furs with their warmth, muted luster and faintly pungent feral reek. They suggested something of an antique brass or golden brown, something moist. But there was no natural smell of any kind on her.

How much do I know about her?

On our trips together, I had seen her emerge from the bathroom. She never bothered to close the door. She was naked save for a towel wrapped tightly into a turban around her head. Her breasts were only slightly bigger than buds. From the waist down to her hips she had the shape of a gourd. Imagine how I felt when I found her as unflustered as the calm light shining down upon her naked body exposed to my scrutiny! She decided to have her breasts lifted after moving in with that man. I related to her the many stories of botched boob jobs. What a stupid idea! She was doing all this for a man, a man with already a double chin who believed politics had nothing to do with life. In those three years of what she believed was love, she devoted every atom of her mind and heart to him. She tried to defend him, saying he had never complained. Then why was she bent on getting the silicone gel-filled breast implants?

Her involvement with that man was just a vague tumult. So many tears were wrung from her eyes because of him. Her eyes seemed forever wet with them no matter how often she wiped them away. Waitresses tiptoed past our table but looked at us in impolite enquiry and met my glaring eye and went away. She didn't seem to have noticed any of that, still sniffling. She picked up a paper napkin and covered her nose with it, blowing her nose into it with a muffled sound.

I want to meet him, I said in an even, gentle tone, I want to let him know how much pain you are in.

She paused her nose blowing and dropped the napkin. With a noticeable forward bending of her back, pale and somewhat alarmed, she looked into my face as if searching for something. She said she would wait outside for me, then got to her feet and left with her head held high. I felt the immaculate white ceiling of the café was coming crashing down to crush me.

We walked home in silence. The silence coalesced like the thickening dusk. When we neared her home she remarked that I was rather like him, in that I was always changing boyfriends. I retorted that at least I never trifled with the affections of others. She said his love for her was genuine. How do you know? I countered. She said it was none of my business and I had no business criticizing her. After sparring for a while, she started crying again. I laid out all my dismal experiences, just for the sake of reminding her that I was once as naïve as she was (it's not strictly accurate. Am I not still as naïve as before?). In the worst episode someone surreptitiously slipped a date rape drug into my drink. I was completely and helplessly at his mercy and the next day I was left to try and accept the fait accompli. Are you sure you didn't drink too much liquor? She asked. I said I didn't. He is too much. Why hasn't he called me yet? Of course she meant that old son of a bitch with a double chin. What is wrong with you? I asked, trying hard to control my emotion. Why are you thinking about him again? Saying nothing, she took out her cell phone and looked at it with a heavy sigh. I decided to shut up and keep my own counsel.

We went back to our respective homes. As I climbed into bed, I was overcome by a sudden weariness. I didn't feel so exhausted on that morning. That morning I woke up to find myself in a huge bed, all ninety pounds of naked flesh weighing down on the rumpled bed sheet. I smelled an odor of dried perspiration coming from my armpits. My colleague was asking me on the phone how the interview went. I could discern puzzlement and even suspicion in her tone. I tried to sound perky. It went very well, I said, I finished it last night in under an hour. I even had time to pay a visit to my mother. That colleague shared an apartment with me. She didn't pursue the subject. Sometime that night I did make a trip to my parents' home. My mother saw me shuffle into the apartment and lackadaisically go into my own little room. She came toward my room and opened the door a crack. But she did not come in, asking through the gap what I wanted for lunch. After a long interval, a slender shaft of light beamed into my little room. I lay in the darkness gazing at the beam of light, which reminded me of a pathway, which I hoped would lead straight to childhood. When I was a kid, Mother always tried to make sure I got a lot of sleep. I enjoyed lying in that low, narrow little bed and listening to the sound made by the sewing machine she was operating downstairs. It was a comforting, reassuring sound—clickety-clack, clickety-clack. That sound prevented thinking and as a result induced sleep. Those faraway times, faraway nights! No one had ever rolled—how I was rolled!—me around like that. Don't you wish to have something to eat? My mother asked again. I did not reply and she retraced her steps to her room.

In the beginning, I was probably no different than most other girls. I paid attention to the hygiene and neatness of my person and keeping smelly odors off my body. I held my breath to suppress a burp or a hiccup. I squeezed my sphincters to suppress gas and flatulence. I turned sideways and bent down to expel mucus from my nose. I fought dandruff with shampoo. I took daily baths. As for the other common leakages fore and aft, they are products of our sadly inescapable humanity. At age twenty a fetus grew in my belly without my realizing it. When I found out its existence my first reaction was one of terror and rejection. Gradually there was a mysterious process of transference. When I was alone, in the street, at night, or in the early morning, I would closely follow its slow growth. I had at first a repugnance of it, because it kept growing, no matter what state I was in, inexorably and mercilessly, with little regard to my circumstances and the terror and anxiety I was going through. Such indiscreet growth doomed it. After it was scraped from the womb I developed a queasy fascination with my body. The fascination rose around me, like the steam in a sauna, and protected my womb. But this body of mine betrayed me, and brought stigma on me, and I became afraid of it. I had never before had this sense of self-disgust. I never again touched that part of my body with my hand.

Can I possibly succeed in my attempt to write a story about me and her on this black machine, with, in my earshot, not the sound of my mother's sewing machine but that of a computer keyboard?

How do you explain the color white to a person who was born blind? F once asked me. I led him onto a snowy field. The color white possessed the attributes of coolness and emptiness. When did I begin to understand these attributes? Not the whole body, but only a part thereof, such as the heart or the brain, was so white, so hollow. It started out as a white dot and grew night after night, until a great deal of feeling was lost to memory. This kind of white evoked the image of me wearing an elegant dress and heavy makeup lying on a brand new bed, surrounded by fresh cut flowers. I felt as if I were in an alfresco plaza, where any and all could approach the bed, some with trembling hands, some icy cold hands, or burning hot hands. Everyone was talking to me at once, their words hammering at my eardrums, causing my ears to buzz. At first I tried to get away from this bed and the crowd surrounding it by reminiscing about certain people. I thought about her, about F, and about my ex-husband, picturing them sleeping peacefully in their respective rooms, safe from these marauding hands, thinking maybe she was still awake like me, looking up wistfully. But she must be thinking of that man; of this I was sure. The bed was becoming worn and rickety, bearing a dilapidated me on it, navigating through the throngs, muffling its creaking.

She told me a lot of things about that man. I often think of those things. He suffered from frequent insomnia. He said he was lonely, didn't like golf, didn't know how to dance cheek to cheek and had absolutely no interest in jazz music. In the winter of his fifth year a little sister was added to the family. His parents were always fighting. At age nine he started cooking for his little sister and telling her stories. The stories usually went like this: in the aftermath of a catastrophe only they survived, and he found her a cave where they were safe and warm.

It was in his office that they made love for the first time. He lifted her skirt (I have seen her limp pink cotton underwear that couldn't keep its shape). The leather sofa got wet. She said her greatest wish was to spend the night with him, lying next to him, being gently undressed by him. She would rest her head on his arm and caress his face with love, sigh contentedly and sink into sleep with him.

Why was he fascinated by her? I do not mean her, my girlfriend, but "her" in the broad sense. What were his esthetic criteria? I know he had a succession of girlfriends and married twice. This heavy-set man did not have any bulging muscles. I try to picture that mass of flab quivering on top of her, in the upright wishbone of her lifted, wide-flung legs, she screaming to the rhythm his movement. Why do people call this making love?

When I had nothing better to do, I would take a stroll in the street in front of her apartment building in hopes of running into that man. Thrashing and rolling in bed, panting endearments, crying out for pleasure as if in pain, titillating that member into tumescence with one's toe or saliva, I knew how to do all that. I slackened my pace as I walked past the green metal gate, hoping to catch him leaving her building. On a few occasions I saw her emerging from her building, her expressionless and bored-looking face blending in with the crowd. Once she actually looked saucy and smart when she had her hair braided and woven into a plait. Finally, my patience was rewarded. My heart started beating wildly when I spotted him. I studied his face, which was pudgy, soft and despicably flushed. Somehow there arose in my mind the image of her bare legs thrusting up at the ceiling. The massive body in a black suit moved away from me. I could only take the opposite direction. On another occasion I saw the two of them come out of the gate, one falling slightly behind, and enter a café restaurant diagonally across the street.

In the end it was through her that I met him. It was easy. While constantly on guard, she didn't consider me a potential threat. That afternoon I was chatting with her in that café restaurant they had previously entered, when he walked in. He dispensed with formalities with me, but merely laid a business card in front of me. I observed her furtively and found her occupied with the pearly gel balls in her milk tea. Just wait and see what would come of it.

Care for some ice cream? The man asked us. He must have a fetish for tongues. Let's show him how we lick! The torch-shaped ice cream was licked down evenly into a shrinking round ball. She ate faster than me and was tearing the paper napkin into strips in suspicion-tinged impatience. The man leaned back in his chair, putting one leg across the other. The little round table stood languidly in the sun. I did not volunteer any conversation, nor did she. The three of us just sat there, and watched the patrons of the café amid the aroma of his recently lit cigarette. Finally his gaze fell on me as he asked me why I called myself Zou Zou. I told him. Is that so? *Zou* means "brisk walk" in ancient Chinese? He played back my explanation. It means the same in Japanese, she added.

Then let us go for a *zou zou*, he said.

We walked slowly up the street on the sidewalk, me and her in front and him behind us. Doesn't he need to work today? I asked her. She ignored the question and said, turning her head around, Zou Zou lives nearby. Why did she have to point that out? So the man asked where my apartment was. I gestured vaguely toward the other side of the street. Down there, I said, it is an old house.

These Western-style old houses are very expensive nowadays, he said, accepting the conventional wisdom. Mine is an old traditional house in an alley. It crawls with slimy slugs. He nodded musingly. My childhood home was a *shikumen*, he said, I had to empty the chamber pots every day until I went to high school. This was no comfort to me. On the contrary, it caused me to have a momentary image of my own one-thousand-yuan-a-month little apartment. I could see that bedroom with a dining table and a computer desk, and even catch a whiff of the damp, musty odor emanating from the base of the north wall.

They saw me to the entrance of my residential compound. We usually take the car. We have done enough walking for one day, she complained. From an apartment way back in the compound the sound of a TV reached our earshot. In the gathering twilight my girlfriend was clinging languidly to him, like a melting toffee candy bar. I went in by myself. Will my first time with him happen in this apartment? There is not much room for maneuver in this cramped space. With my head thrown back and my chest thrust out, he appeared in eager anticipation, I can use my sharp teeth to bite him until his eyes burn with desire. I can perhaps try my toe, sliding it along the inner side of his calf all the way to his crotch, although my calves are not shapely enough.

She and I were polar opposites. Unlike me, she had a perfect figure for dresses. They just fitted her like a glove. But her arms and legs were too stiff. I saw her dance and practice yoga. She reminded me of a Clockwork Man coming abruptly to life. Her laughter had a muffled quality to it while I laughed, rather cackled, like a hen. La—dy! I would imitate her wearied, angry tone and then burst out cackling at my imitation. The idea of living in her shoes had never occurred to me before, but now it sent a palpable thrill through me. I wished to caress the man that she had caressed, to somehow know intimately, from the inside, as it were, what his body was like, its different parts, different smells, different urges. How, how would it be? I itched to know! In an overcast afternoon on a work day—here I leap ahead—we did it in a hotel room. He went at it over me for a few minutes and I emitted muffled moans, or was it suppressed laughter? So this is how your body looks and feels like, he remarked, I want to know more of it. I was eager to know how he felt when he did it with her. He replied, without thinking, that she got wet much sooner than me. As if to fill the silence occasioned by his comment, he added, but you two are different. This blurted-out secret did not put me to shame. I blushed only because it was an unflattering commentary on her that she was perceived to be too easily aroused by him.

I wondered if she knew that there was now an extra

bond between her and me. We shared that medium, which acted like the thin silvery trail left overnight by a slug linking the sinks of two adjoining households. Soon we began to have similar thoughts and feelings. At night, in bed under the blanket, I would think of the same man as she did. She no longer needed to tell me things about him, for I would know all about them myself.

She would, as she had always enjoyed doing, affectionately slip her arm through mine and share with me their little secrets. I found that kind of zeal a bit odd. I tried to avoid her. I couldn't stand being alone with her. She often came to find me after he had left, when her body was still quietly and offensively giving off a faint fleshy stink, of flesh recently rubbed and softened by that man. I couldn't say anything about it to her. But the odor distressed me. I wished I would have a rambunctious little boy in the future, who liked to make a racket when he played with his toys. Then I would deal with him like Mother. I would snatch the toy from him and fling it out of the high-floor window, the toy making a loud rattling sound as it tumbled down.

That man adopted an ambiguous attitude with

us. On the few occasions when the three of us had dinner together, he appeared distracted, but she was like an overripe apple, cloyingly sweet, stopping eating from time to time to cast a contented glance at him. She was so happy she instinctively furrowed her eyebrows. Then she would start chuckling to herself. The man would talk about his work at the table, throwing out jargon at a fast clip. It sounded less like a conversation than a monologue and all she did was fixing her eyes on him admiringly. Yet I understood well enough what it was he was trying to say, and often before he was halfway through trying to say it, I was sure she never read the financial pages, which only made me more impatient and irritated with her.

I kept a cat when I was a child. It was a frisky little tabby, of which I was greatly fond. When there were no adults about, I would stand on the landing of the stairs and tease it with a stalk of hay. When I wiggled the stalk, the cat would pitch forward only to tumble nimbly head over heel and leap to his feet again after taking a few steps, this time to a greater height. This would go on until it got dizzy and started mewing piteously. What a vulnerable little being! I got very emotional. When it finally flopped on the floor, too exhausted to continue the game, I would nudge it with my toe until it vanished from my sight.

As a matter of fact when I ran into that man again after the formal introduction at the café restaurant, and spoke to him, he didn't remember who I was. Nor did he invite me to any place for a chat. He was wearing a light blue checkered shirt. He paused in the street and took a friendly look at me, apparently recognizing me but not remembering my name. It was only at the fourth chance meeting that we sat down together, just the two of us. Didn't she come with you? He asked. He also asked me if I cared for something to drink. I asked for a glass of fresh-squeezed orange juice. Why don't we, he spoke with an ambiguous familiarity, order some desserts? I shook my head. It wouldn't be long before I would get into this man's bed (I knew this for a fact). I was excited but at the same time, I also felt sorry for her. He would "penetrate" me, and in turn I would "punch a hole" through her heart, just as she had left a "hollowness" in my heart when she was being "penetrated" by him. It would be a vicious cycle. I cocked my head, buoyed by that thought. I must have looked like a silly woman poised to plunge into love, for he laid his hand over mine, a tremor passing through his fingertips for some obscure reason.

What was she doing in her apartment? Was she telling the nanny to make a stew or soup for him? That would be hilarious. I had tasted those concoctions originally meant for him. They were topped by floating golden slicks of cooking oil and as the spoon skimmed the surface it stirred up a pleasant aroma. Little did she know that he was spending this time with me here, before we tumbled into bed, before the phone rang from his wife. In anticipation of the man's visit, my girlfriend would try on one dress after another. That nanny just couldn't keep her mouth shut. It wouldn't occur to my girlfriend that right at this moment and right under her nose he was with me across the street. The man's hand started to inch up my hand. The sun, filtered by the window glass, felt so ardent. Little fellow! Where did you come from? The man muttered to himself. My back was bathed in sunlight. It felt as though she was watching us from her balcony window on a high floor. The sunlight was kept outside my body. As I wrote down these lines, my memory groped in search of details. Sunlight would not penetrate the placid gloom of this little north-facing room.

The afternoon after she obtained her marriage certificate, I handed her the wedding gift I picked for her, and with smiling eyes and a cheery expression, I asked about her husband. It was one of those days when summer was at its hottest. Residual pimples from an acne outbreak were visible on her face and her hair had a greasy, unwashed look. Folds of flab at her waist quivered under her flimsy synthetic T-shirt. She showed me the diamond ring on her finger, with that unfocused look in her eyes, as if she were not quite persuaded of its authenticity. I brought myself closer to her. She smelled like a completely changed woman.

That fat, thickset man came before me after having duly cleansed himself of his sweaty, greasy smell and the residual cigarette stench. Be nice to yourself! So I let her appear before us. She was pale but wholly real. She looked at me with despair in her eyes, and tried desperately to stop me. Under the weight of that man, I was subjugated, penetrated, rolled and variously repositioned. I wrapped my arms around her body in a lock. Her face, on fire, was turned toward me. Her lover was eating her in mouthfuls. There was a wet penetration. The man's forehead was dripping with perspiration. I turned to bury my face in the bed, bearing the brunt of her churning wrath. That fury swirled in my body, just as it happened every time I stood beside her, thirsting to take her in my arms but stopping short, letting the moment slip away. They seemed to be everywhere and nowhere. I broke into sobs and moans, loud and beyond all control.

Sometimes I would wake up in the middle of the night and see her face hovering near the ceiling, with her mouth gaping wide, as if in a shout, or ready to devour me. There was always a faint light in the room. Once, possibly hoping to provoke her into swooping down from the ceiling to rough me up, I picked up a book and hurled it toward the ceiling. Her face dissolved quietly.

It was my mother who realized something was the matter with me. She told me to see her, but said nothing to me. I would have preferred an interrogation, followed by a smack as happened in the far past. My mother only slapped me once. She left immediately after administering it and slammed the door after her. She couldn't fathom why I had done it. She said she hated me. I wonder if she recognized my love for her. To this day I cannot be sure that she did.

Things happened without warning.

I felt an unaccountable disgust whenever I thought of the rabid anger my mother exhibited that once. It was like wearing woolen clothes over one's bare skin, or wearing a thick coat of honey on one's face and having strands of hair trapped in it. It snowed again. I have always been strongly susceptible to the weather and its effects. I chose the occupation of a writer because I disliked having to leave my home on inclement days. I am thankful that I could listen to weather forecasts in an air-conditioned room and imagine other people struggling with the elements. This is one of the blessings of my life.

My stepfather once asked me what I wanted to be when I grew up. Could he have imagined what I have become? I am sitting in a chair, by the small square table that served as my mother's dining table, and basking quietly in a room temperature of eighteen degrees Celsius in this first month of the year. From the moment he found out he had cancer of the pancreas, he was gnawed by anxiety day and night until his death. I wonder if hell is like winter, with sunlight retiring early, leaving only sleepless darkness. There he could only sleep a comatose sleep, never to wake up.

She visited me before deciding to get married. We lay next to each other. She talked through the night, as if driven by a dynamo inside her. She alternately sobbed and chuckled in the dark, for the heartlessness and cruelties visited upon her. Most of the night, she lay on her side curled up, clutching her pillow. Hand in hand, we reminisced about the day we first met. When I stepped into that noisy, smoke-filled banquet room that day, you were the first person to catch my eye. I don't mean you had stunning looks; you just looked different from all the girls I had known. You sat among the men, not talking to anyone. But I could see that you were trying to seduce them in your own way. You had a head of curly hair and a way of dreamily twisting a lock of hair around a finger. That was a sure way to make the men think you were weaving dreams. Even though another girl was much prettier than you, I decided I'd rather sit closer to you. This was how she recalled our first meeting. Ah, those parties, so many of them in those days. I was struggling to make my mark as a writer at the time. I had given thought to what kind of people I needed to know. I tried my damnedest to make myself attractive. I knew how people always picked fruit that possessed alluring exteriors at the fruit stall. More than one man noticed me, and one took me to his apartment. He had a spacious apartment in a high rise. He showed me with great pride his commodious study, lined floor to ceiling with books, requiring the help of a ladder. I was very young and somewhat naïve then. I can't imagine why I found myself in that apartment. He reeled off the names of women writers who had benefited from his recommendations, or so he believed. He left the choice to me. He turned on me a gaze of flawless candour. Let's have something to eat first, he suggested. I was treated to a hot pot dinner and was able to wriggle out of the awkward situation without too much difficulty.

We talked all night. All through that night, we were like two travelers hastening along a dusty trail, hoping a clean high road would come into sight when we turned the next corner. When birds started chirping and dawn broke, her hand came to rest on my waist as we lay facing each other. Her eyes fell on my pajamas and she started fiddling with a round button on them; in her customary coy and peremptory manner she demanded my presence at her wedding.

The wedding was held in a garden somewhere. It was only a few days after the advent of autumn, so the sunlight still dazzled the eyes and the air felt like it had been sprinkled with some desiccant. Taxis and private cars kept pulling up in front of the garden hotel and soon the lawn filled up with people, women in lipstick and men in dress shirts. Jewelry glittered on her head. Nobody got drunk. The wedding concluded with her being carried by the bridegroom to their room.

That afternoon when my mother gave me a slap on the face, I was so angry and disgusted I wanted to run away from home. I won't care, she said. Get you out from under my feet. I moved back to the little hovel in a shantytown, forgoing the amenities of a self-flushing toilet or a bathroom. All I had in the room was a stove burning coal bricks. I befriended girls who lived also in shantytowns. Not long after that I made the acquaintance of an elderly man, who lived in a nice apartment and wore wire-frame glasses. I received books and manuscript paper from him as gifts. One weekend he took me to the botanical garden. He led me through mostly deserted trails in the garden where I was dwarfed by the trees. Sometimes we walked abreast of each other, sometimes I fell back a step behind him. I had a premonition of something sinister happening and was even a little afraid. But he merely sat down on a lawn and offered me a banana. He watched me finish it and said, with fatigue written all over his face, all right, let's go home. From then on I no longer went out in search of diversions but focused on my studies. When I needed diversions I would catch some flies, put them in a plastic bag and place it over my desk lamp to watch with fascination their desperate movements.

In high school, I had a college student for a pen pal. Our first meeting took place on his campus. He wore a sleeveless sweater and I could see clearly the black stubble under his armpits. The second time we dated, I took him to the botanical garden, on a sudden impulse to play a game of chase with him (inspired, I think, by the novels of Chiung Yao). I ran in different directions in the wooded area. It was not a clear day. It was overcast and gray. He tried to catch me. I tried to evade his pursuit, all the while laughing. Finally he caught up with me and we tangled together. I kicked at him, but he grabbed my wrist and twisted my arm behind my back. I had no choice but to surrender immediately. My wrist still red from his grip, I started to run again in joyous abandon, only to land in a pond, which was so completely covered with duckweed that I had taken it for just another lawn. The pond was only knee deep. Feeling defeated and frustrated, I bit hard on my lower lip and my face drew into an unhappy frown. There, there! He jumped into the water too, now we are equal. I felt a little chilly and leaned against a tree trunk. He pressed his leg against mine. This way you'll feel warmer, he flushed to his ears as he explained.

I once lay on my side in a bed and looked languidly at a man. I learned how to look out the window without expression, with my head resting on a hand. Sometimes when I curled up one leg, those hands would creep along the inner side of my calf until they reached my knee. I would not allow them to go any further. Therefore, they would seek out other areas—modest mounds sheathed in white or pink cotton. In those years, time seemed to have slowed. I felt unhurried, until that morning when I woke up to find myself in a big bed. I smelled an odor of dried perspiration coming from my armpits. It was proof that my body had been repeatedly used. Sweat poured out of every pore, turning my skin clammy and wet. After a couple of minutes of bafflement, I walked into the bathroom.

All of a sudden, I was seized by a sense of bitterness and fury. I washed myself clean, without tarrying in front of the mirror. The previous evening, before I left home, I looked fresh like a tree-ripe fruit in the mirror, filled with sweet expectations and having no premonition of landing in a pickle. Nobody expects bad things to happen to oneself, but what will be will be.

Her bridegroom and she still met quite often with me. Mostly we whiled the time away in a restaurant. I was not a good conversationalist and the moment they sat down they started arguing. They effortlessly switched topics, from stocks to cars, and I fell to listening and nodding at appropriate moments. I could pass the entire evening without uttering a single word. Silence could sometimes be a form of showing off; keeping quiet often induced more talk in others. The two of them would yak until it was time to close up, when both were exhausted and even the waiters' patience was worn thin.

After many such boring dinners, the husband began to take a curious interest in me. That evening she had to take a call, so she excused herself and went out. She was on the phone for fifteen or thirty minutes, pacing back and forth between two trees outside the restaurant. The food was getting cold, and a film of hard fat formed on the surface, effectively deterring further use of the chopsticks. I kept twirling my cup, without making a sound; I noticed he had been eyeing me all this while. Let's not wait for her. He said it on purpose. He poured tea for me. I dropped my napkin and when I bent down to pick it up, my hair fell smoothly over one shoulder. When I straightened up, she was walking back in. I looked at her, this woman pacing the street at night. Who was it? You talked quite a while on the phone. The husband instinctively arched his back like a wary animal. It was nothing. It was something to do with the office. The lies may have started that evening or much earlier. They would spread like a wild fire. I had a feeling she was observing me.

I have not yet described the husband. F once said that my understanding of men would be ridiculed by men. Husbands, married men as lovers and single men exhibit no significant outward differences, as far as I am concerned. They may have different ages, hairstyles and bone structures. They may be clumsy or deft, have prominent ears or not, a long nail on the pinkie or not, that's all. The husband had a small build, average size ears and irregular teeth. Once I saw a sliver of green vegetable leaf stuck in his front teeth (when in contact with saliva, food particles turned a sickly gray). He had a passably high forehead (a sign of shrewdness?). With every step he took his entire body would heave upward and he walked with his feet splayed outward. That's as far as my general impression of him goes. Tolerance, he said to me that evening, is easier said than done. It takes a lifetime of practice.

So then he had to tolerate the fickleness of her affection. That married man, just when I was on the verge of forgetting him, made another foray into my life and her life. In my home she described what that old man said on the phone. He said his heart ached for her. That was no love or admiration, but only a sexual impulse. No, I couldn't bring myself to tell her that in such stark terms. She would once again allow her entire being to slip into the hands of that man. Then would follow a "stormy passion" (I am sure she would use such terms smacking of literary aesthetics), and the inevitable, renewed profession of love. Handholding, embraces and declarations of love, all that happened also between him and me. I remember the day he removed the last stitch of clothing from my body and I shivered with cold as I waited for him. Why didn't I feel love then, that so-called love?

Her secret escapades went on sub rosa. When would her husband suspect, find out?

But it was in those days that she surprised me with a kiss. It was our first kiss. It happened on the sofa in my apartment. A kiss between a man and a woman can lead to many things. But a kiss between two women with normal sexual orientations can only be in the past tense. The apartment I rented was on the street level. In the garden shared with my neighbor his half was densely populated by plants, while my half was a few square meters of fallow land. The door leading to the garden was a French window covered with long curtains. One afternoon she and I were sitting on my sofa looking out at the garden that offered nothing worth seeing when suddenly she gripped my hands and touched her lips to mine, breathing a sweet, fresh scent into my mouth. I couldn't do a thing. I was nonplused and indescribably tense. The lips slowly shifted their focus. Her lips were gentle and soft, warm but not moist, almost insubstantial.

After my stepfather's passing, his biological daughter

claimed his apartment. My mother asked me to help her move out. That residential compound was hopelessly outdated. There were only me and my mother in the apartment. I was relaxed and did not feign sorrow to humor her. The place felt empty and although that daughter was not there, something ice cold lingered in the air. I couldn't tell if my mother still loved me. Before his passing, she had a good life in this apartment and I had tried to sabotage it.

The apartment was not much different from the one in my memory, but appeared smaller. There was that rosewood dining table, on which my mother used to lay out a few dishes to go with the morning porridge for him. He was quite finicky about details. The dishes had to be arranged in a pleasing pattern. The utensils had to be matching sets. Sugar must be added to the fermented bean curd. Peanuts and seaweed must be fried the day they were to be consumed. Napkins were needed for an ornamental purpose. Then there was that spacious rosewood bed, their bed. I bet the man's previous wife had slept in it. The sight of my mother bent over the bed packing her clothes evoked memories of the days when she bent over the bathtub scrubbing it. She was a little out of breath, but her backside calmly bore the brunt of the scrutiny of my stepfather, who fussed about the hairs I left on the walls above the bathtub. I am bored to death here, I complained, but my mother was satisfied. She had found herself a nice place to stay here. Why don't you come live with us? She said, but you'll have to learn to behave yourself better. So the hallway was converted into my little room, but I couldn't stand the way she looked at the man those days. She was like a prostitute in ancient times, solicitous and obsequious. She bustled about, squatting on her heels to wash the man's feet. Whenever a scowl appeared on the man's face, she would put down her chopsticks in the middle of her meal. I had no use for a mother like that. The sight of her wiping off the water I splashed all over the bathroom afforded me a vindictive pleasure. But her posture of raised backside filled me with distress. I would really have loved to give her a piece of my mind.

I saw photos of my mother in her younger days. She had been small and frail like a wraith. When she read, there was a serene quality to her face. She offered herself to a man seventeen years her senior, who wore a denture, kept the nail of his pinkie long (supposedly to serve as an ear pick), and enjoyed spending an inordinate amount of time watching a woman cleaning his apartment. I've lost count of how many times my mother had scrubbed his bathtub and his toilet bowl. The chores never seemed to end. I imagined him losing his footing in that big slippery, white bathtub and then all would be quiet. For me as well as for my mother I wanted it all to be over with. But my mother always breached the quiet and would knock on the bathroom door every ten minutes, only to hear a heave of water on the other side of the door. Sometimes she would ask to rub his back with a towel. My room did not have a door and directly faced the bathroom. I could only try to shut out all thoughts. Now that he died, all of that died with him.

My mother did not tell me about the few months he was in the hospital. He was terrified by his cancer of the pancreas. Maybe other patients shared his room. So many years of her life were packed into a few cardboard boxes. She appeared very tired, so tired that she had no energy left to hate me.

After that kiss that felt passionless and unreal, she asked me to accompany her to see that man. We went to a bar that began to fill with patrons only in the evening. The man was there. He had chosen a spot far from the door. We sat down on the sofa. Order whatever you like, she said. I ordered lemon juice with honey. It came in a very tall glass. I listened distractedly to their conversation and pulped the lemon slices with silent stabs of the straw. Pieces of pulp floated in the liquid, clouding it up. The place was almost deserted. A young girl stood behind the bar counter, her head forever bent over whatever she was doing. Her hair had been dyed a yellow; she had a nice figure but she was not particularly good-looking. Another girl, wearing a black uniform, stood in a far corner with her hands clasped behind her, watching the entrance. The door was wide open, letting in a fat slab of pale sunlight that landed softly near her feet. That kiss (I've been trying to relive that sensation) had a vague tenderness about it. After that kiss, the two little girls should be lying demurely in bed, a sheet unfurling and falling over them. But now, it was that man lying there instead. The man seized her hand, the hand on the table; the other hand was holding the drink. Her fingers were a little on the plump and stubby side, with no grace to speak of. It suddenly reminded me of my mother's hands. With those kinds of hands, she was only good for groaning and moaning. Girls with long, slender fingers will put up a token resistance. Late, too late! She yelled at the man.

By the time we left the bar it was already night, and time to have dinner with her husband. The husband didn't seem to sense anything and made no comment about her spending the entire afternoon with me. Would he have cared more if he had seen how she had cast amorous glances at the fat old man in the privacy of that room? In love, it is said, the heartless one usually gets to claim the title to nobility. He didn't know the evening would end like this: his heart brimming with happiness, he looked at his pretty wife lying on the big bed, kissing that face, again and again, kissing the face that had been kissed by others.

Have I ever really fallen in love with anybody?

I was 15 when my mother gave me a smack in the face. Shortly after that incident, when summer vacation came around, I went alone to my uncle's home in another town. In those two months I was capricious, if not cavalier, with the physically well-developed boys of the town. It was fun. Even to this day when I think back to those months, I still find it great fun. For example, I would crumple a sheet of paper into a ball and throw it at that boy reading on a reclining chair. They all treated me as a naïve young girl from Shanghai, except that boy, who rarely deigned to look at me. I kept throwing paper balls at him. Finally one day he jumped up and glared angrily at me. I grabbed his sweat shirt and pulled him down to my height, and kissed him. He began to gladly put up with me and followed meekly behind me. I took total liberties with his lips and tongue. Once I kissed him with such force that his lips were crushed against my front teeth and my mouth filled with a faint taste of blood. He pushed me away with a scowl. On a muggy afternoon my uncle was playing mahjong with other members of his family in the sitting room downstairs and I was taking a nap in my bed. He sneaked up the back stairs to take a peek at me. I took him in my arms and allowed him to fondle me. Then I gave him a gentle slap in the face to stop his marauding hands. He reddened to the roots of his hair, appearing ecstatic and pained at the same time. But soon I was bored. I didn't know what I was going to do with him. He was still tentatively feeling my body here and there. I gripped his balls, tightened my fist around them and started yanking them. He yelped with pain. I let go, and he sat up, rubbing his crotch, stupefied. The room became very quiet, but nothing happened after that. He toddled off.

I have always disliked being photographed. The traditional SLR camera is an uncanny invention. It carries out surveillance with a single eye and mocks the struggles of people to look like someone else. I don't mind the point-and-shoot cameras that have become popular. They are easier to placate and docilely accept whatever image they capture of their subject. They are not inquisitive and not unsettling. Observing, spying and searching for hidden truths makes me feel like a wild animal tracking down its prey.

After my stepfather's death, my mother moved in with me. She began to fear death. She boiled all her vegetables in water, adding almost no salt. She did the same with fried eggs. I had to buy a collection of seasonings to spice up my meals. My mother totally ignored this silent protest of mine. Soon I rented another apartment for myself and went back to visit her once a month. She never turned on the air conditioner. She kept the living room window open a crack even on snowy days, to vent any leaked cooking gas. She kept the lights burning bright though. She spent a lot of time watching TV from the sofa. In the room in which I used to live she planted aloe vera in a number of pots. On New Year's Eve I called to ask her if she was willing to come out the next day to have dinner with me. She said she would rather not go out, adding that restaurant food was unclean and one could get diarrhea from it. You are such an eccentric, I said. I am indeed an eccentric, and I gave birth to an eccentric junior, she retorted.

My mother was not like this in her younger days. When I was a child, she often took me to the park on Zhaojiabang Road, where the shadows and light under the trees were soft and subdued and the plants luxuriant and lush. For a time I suffered from a strange disorder, which caused me to trip without warning when I ran. My mother believed it could be alleviated with "black (Polyrachis) ant powder." And morning after morning, she would sit under some tree catching ants with a pair of tweezers. On Sunday afternoons she would wash my hair. One autumn afternoon, I well remember, she made me bend over in a standing posture. With my hair cascading over my eyes, she poured water from a thermos bottle brought down to a comfortable temperature over the top of my head. After drying my hair with a towel she told me to sit in the sun and started shelling "Xinchangfa" (well-known Shanghai food brand) *tangchao lizi* (chestnuts roasted in sand with brown sugar).

At age ten I discovered my mother's secret. When she took me to the park, there would be a man waiting there. I played not far from them, alone, abandoned by my mother. But he was laughing, as he said something to my mother, all the while glancing in my direction. Whatever he was saying made her laugh too. It always ended the same way in those clear, sunny days. The man turned to leave and she started toward me. When she tried to take my hand, I would immediately thrust it into my pocket. Then she would promise to get me something delicious to eat and, insinuating a hand into the crook of my arm and with a series of soft tugs, made me come with her. By the time we reached the Qiaojiazha Family Restaurant, my mood had returned to its former cheerfulness.

Thus, in the year I graduated elementary school, my mother was divorced. I did not feel its impact at the time.

My mother became shameless after remarrying. My stepfather would sit cross-legged, reading his *Xinmin Evening News*, and tapping all the while an annoying rhythm on the desk with his long-nailed pinkie. My mother would serve tea to him and he would take it from her hands. Nothing appeared out of the ordinary. At night they locked the master bedroom door. In the darkness I couldn't detect any indecent sounds of intimacy, only occasional snatches of indistinct, whispered words. Wild imaginations haunted me. They were both very thin, but thin people, no less than fat ones, could be vulgarly united. During the day I would watch for any chance to hold my mother's eyes with mine, but she merely looked at me with a puzzled look, unflinching and unenthusiastic.

I slept with him, I told her. She listened without seeming to register it. After a while, she loudly called out his name, in disbelief. She appeared shocked, but her reaction was not at all what I had expected. She did not act out her anger. She could understandably have slapped me, but she didn't. That was unsettling to me. So I felt compelled to further provoke her. He is one and a half times as old as we are. He has a sizable paunch and a hairy chest to boot. How could you have accepted someone like him? She instantly assumed a condescending attitude. Did you tell him you loved him? Did he tell you he loved you? Did he arouse you? It was she who had gleefully fallen into the arms of that fat man, and now she had the cheek to show contempt for me! Had she accepted the new state of affairs so calmly? She could very well have clawed my face, like a kitten, with her polished nails. Go away! I don't ever want to see your face again! She said, with her eyes directed at the table and the shrillness of her voice suppressed and trapped in her throat. She didn't say "I hate you" or things like that.

That was, so far, our last exchange of words.

Everything is so quiet, as if she never came into my life. I cannot hear her voice. Why has she not come back to haunt me, with her constant phone calls? Why this silence day after day, night after interminable night? It is like the snow of this winter that has been swept to a corner and just stays there. When we pass it by, we no longer see its original whiteness, but it refuses to melt. Not a word. A solid wall of silence.

I do not want to be alone like this.

This is an indescribably dismal winter. According

to the papers, this is the first real snow since the delivery of Shanghai from KMT control. Such quiet and gloomy days remind me of another time, in a far past. It was a year day temperatures just reached twenty-five degrees Celsius early in the summer. I pulled up my blouse over my head in front of him and took it off. He put down his newspaper. He had never really looked at me before. I was not fully prepared, but I thought I couldn't retreat now. He did not do anything but kept his eyes on me. My skirt dropped to the floor. It was a little chilly and I got goose bumps. I felt numb all over and my ears became momentarily deaf. His cough awakened me out of my reverie. He was slipping through my fingers! I reached out a hand and grabbed his wrist. Both of us were petrified with fright. Put your clothes back on! This is unbecoming! He murmured under his breath. With a jerk he freed himself from my grip and bent down to pick up my clothes. I heard the door open and turned to look. My mother was standing in the doorway, the key in her hand. She looked more like a stranger passing through.

Writing

1

The book I really should be writing is one about experiencing yoga. It would start with an explanation of how the book idea came about. I would probably argue the importance of "paying to sweat." It goes without saying that it would be laced with romantic interludes, none of which, I guarantee you, would have anything to do with my own life. As for the size of the first print run, the publisher has agreed to at least thirty thousand. They are still waiting for the book. I intend to make the editors wait some more. Editors are generally patient, I think. So I will write this novella first and leave that other book for later.

The idea of writing this novella came to me on the afternoon of September 25. The gentleman who alerted me to a contest of novellas planned for next year is not a co-worker. He has an office next to mine. He walked in, planted himself by my desk and gave me that piece of information. Hey, your mind is wandering again, my boyfriend said to me. I was thinking about my novella when we were having supper.

In this novella of forty thousand words, I intend to devote some space to the description of my class teachers, whose strict enforcement of rigid discipline was at the origin of my earth-shaking (so I had believed) rebellion during puberty. I will describe how one of them once pushed me with such force that the content of my book bag spilled out and scattered on the ground. She had no idea that a few of the spilled items had been stolen from a small store. The first day I stole an orange. After I'd been stealing for a week, the fat old lady keeping watch on a stool began eyeing me with increasing suspicion. I was afraid that she would inform on me to my mother, who would not fail to give me such a beating that I would smart for days. I decided to take a different road to school, giving a wide berth to the store. Once I injured my face when I fell in a fight and was taken to Zhongshan Hospital by my gym teacher. I asked the doctor not to notify my mother. I ended up receiving seven stitches on my right cheek, and was led home by a teary Mother. I had never thought my mother capable of crying. To project a cool image, I dressed either all in white or all in black and wore prescription sunglasses with a beehive design. When I realized I was always relegated to the last but one row because of my shortness, I became disconsolate. I could start with my first grade class teacher, who, despite the disappointment in my face, refused to let me join the class on a river cruise on the Huangpu because she considered my family too poor to afford it. A few nights ago I happened to be in that neighborhood and decided to take a stroll. Female voices blared over the loudspeaker from time to time calling on the tourists to board their cruise boats for a tour of the river. Those were old steamboats. Further from the riverbank, in the middle of the river a few ships lumbered by like pregnant women clumsily crossing a street. In the meantime, beggars and peddlers dogged me with their wares. Are you trying to write a memoir? Will these unpleasant memories create any significant literary impact? To give the impression of being vindictive and never forgetting a wrong is not very becoming, I nodded, signaling agreement with my boyfriend.

I wrote much in memory of my childhood that egregiously failed to outrage conventional sensibilities. When my mother found out I gave detailed descriptions in my book of how she meted out corporal punishment to me, her beatific expression was undisturbed. Spare the rod and spoil the child, she chirped cheerfully. You see now you'll never run out of grist for your writing mill. That's not far from the truth, for I can go on forever once I start on the subject of my mother's art and science of corporal punishment. Hitting three centimeters below the buttocks inflicts the most pain without injuring muscle or bone. It is therefore the ideal spot for applying the rod. When administering this kind of punishment, the child should lie face down on a long bench and refrain from wriggling or budging lest the force applied fall unevenly. On a number of occasions my mother shared her experience in the matter with neighborhood mothers, all of whom nodded vigorously in approval of her method. You are invading my privacy, I protested. Go ahead and file for the annulment of your adoption papers then! My mother knew where the courts were located. I knew only the hot line number for teenage psychological counseling. Can I dissolve the adoption by making a declaration in the paper? Well, you'll have to pay for that. I didn't have the money. I stalked out of our home in indignation. I headed to the median gardens, where I led a gang of young kids in giving a beating to another gang by hurling small stones at them before heading home in an exultant mood. My mother hit me in public once when I was in middle school. I finished my homework faster than most, and when classmates asked to borrow it in order to copy from it, I never hesitated in handing my homework to them. When my mother learned of it, she slapped me in front of all the students and faculty at the school gate. I vowed on the spot to never speak to her ever again. It took only two days for me to forget my vow. I am fine with it if you give your new novella the title of *On the Receiving End of the Rod*. My mother is nothing if not supportive.

But I have in mind a work that defies prediction. In this work I have no intention of indulging in literary devices. I will not, as I did several years ago, give untrammeled vent to long-suppressed emotions. In that period, stories ran riot in my mind, with no rhyme or reason. Since falling in love with the nouveau roman (new novel) genre of France, my stories have cooled faster than my pen. With the passage of time, I have become more demanding about my writing environment. There will be no shortage of people to interrupt me and distract me as I engage in painstaking wordsmithing. Thus, every morning after ten thirty (just when I am poised to dive into my writing), someone learning the violin on my floor would start playing gracelessly but persistently the same few bars of a tune. This would continue off and on until three in the afternoon. In my imagination the violin player assumes the shape of a chubby five-year-old boy. How could he possibly hope to become a future violinist? My boyfriend likes the playing though. He had wished to learn the piano as a child, but his mother sent him to a judo class instead, to have him out of her sight, I believe, so that his noisy play would not ruin her mood for cooking. At that time she still possessed a pretty face and a nice figure. Soon after her divorce with her first husband, who was a black man, she married a French compatriot of hers. She never thought of making her dark-skinned mixed-blood daughter a violinist. As for her younger son, judo was obviously a good way to wear down his excess energy. I have nothing against the violin, but I'd rather see it only in the context of literary works! Let them go to a concert if they want to listen to the *Liang Zhu (Butterfly Lovers)* Violin Concerto! How am I supposed to write when I am surrounded by noise? I said petulantly. Writing is the only thing you care about. You don't love me, and will not be a good mother in the future. I won't contradict these comments made by my boyfriend in protest. You love yourself more than anyone else. I remember this past observation of my mother's. If I have a child, will I make an exception for him? But that's in the distant future. The person I'd rather wish away is my boyfriend. He is too passionate about music (in compensation for what he missed as child), and he recently bought a guitar. From five in the afternoon I become the captive audience of the slow and sensual French love songs sung by him to his guitar. Sometimes he would start playing video games in the living room the moment he gets home from work. He punches and kicks with the control stick, brandishes his sword and empties his gun. He has to keep firing at the monster wielding an axe until he blows his brains out before the monster is officially terminated. Why can't he have gardening or raising fish for a hobby? One evening he talked about his life on a farm before he was eighteen. They raised cows and sheep and cultivated herbs on the farm. His mother milked the cows to make cheese. The following day I brought him containers of thyme and rosemary. My older sister's name is Rosemary, he told me. By the end of two months those fragrance-dispensing green leaves had withered en masse.

The best solution is for me to move out, or for him to find another place to stay. But relocation is a pain in the neck. Even if I moved out, things would soon go back to where they stand now. Before becoming friends with him, I could sit before a simple white computer desk for hours at a stretch and I could easily write thousands of words a day. Not long after making his acquaintance, I went by myself to Huaihai Road to buy several pairs of high-heeled sandals, a few silk one-piece dresses and some smart-looking sleeveless sweaters. I was not flush with cash, but I seriously splurged for a few weeks. Summer barely started before we came close to parting ways. His former girlfriend had decided to come to China to rekindle their old flame with him, and, citing penury, refused to take a nearby one-bedroom apartment he had found for her but instead moved into his apartment comprising two bedrooms and a living room. For a week, nobody came to my place to interrupt my writing. I began to have sleepless nights. I didn't think that woman could reclaim him, au contraire. But truth is, I must admit my self-confidence was not that shatterproof at the time. I began browsing Web articles about the Aquarius personality. According to some, Aquarius men do not easily change their mind once they decide on a woman. Others assert that Aquarius men have a nostalgic attachment to past relationships.

I was tossed between extremes of euphoria and anguish; finally I decided to close all the web pages I was reading.

I began to seek the protection of my talisman, which I had bought at a painter friend's antique store in Dali. I nearly had a falling-out with a best friend at the time of the purchase, but she lent me the four thousand yuan in the end. It was made from nephrite and featured a walled fortress surrounded by a wide moat and a tiger crouching on the battlement. The painter friend told me that both "tiger" (pronounced *hu*) and "lake" (*hu*) were auspicious symbols because they are phonetically close to "fortune" (*fu*). I lay supine in my bed with the good luck charm clutched tightly in my palm and prayed that it visit endless argument on that man and that woman. He had once told me he felt a deep revulsion whenever she got into a fight with him and he was slapped by her once.

Two weeks later, I can't recall the day of the week, she packed all the clothes and shoes she had toted into that little room and headed to the airport. He didn't lend her a hand, because he was working. The night before, he had told her one more time that he was certain he no longer loved her. He swore to me that he had stayed by himself every single night in the other room of his apartment. She left a small orange yellow bottle, which he continued to use to shape, mold and hold his hair in place. She left some other odds and ends. Obviously I would only be moved to throw them out when I totally lost my head. A month later I casually mentioned the subject of noise. It would be like sleeping on the sidewalk! I gestured toward that high rise standing at the corner.

We looked at different apartments for three days before moving into this apartment on the twenty-eighth floor. It was the most expensive model in the building. Because of our arrangement of sharing expenses, I was not enthusiastic about the choice, but in the end I decided to sign the lease. We were seduced by its quiet ambiance. The apartment I previously rented was situated in a relatively recent housing project in an alley. It had a small bedroom and a large living room that looked out, through four French windows, on a courtyard enclosed by a concrete fence. The lack of trees in the yard was compensated for by its openness to the blue sky. How I missed it! I've been through quite a few rental apartments, including—horror!—a three-month stay in a room with an oversized portrait of a deceased person. Once I rented an apartment that came with an attic. I recouped the rent by subletting the apartment and stuffing myself into the cramped space of the attic, making it my humble home. But it was in that garret that I completed two books. It was the height of stupidity to have given up the single life for love. My landlady was overjoyed when I canceled my lease, because she could charge the new tenant three hundred yuan more per month. It has since been refurnished and become the happy hearth of a family of three. They could not know that my high school first love grew up in a second-floor apartment in the opposite building. Here, I'm going to devote a few paragraphs to him. He ran all the way to my building as soon as he learned from the public service bulletins on TV that I had been admitted to Fudan University after the national college entrance examination. In the alley between buildings, a pot of flowers fell from a balcony to land a few inches from his feet (a typhoon had just passed through Shanghai). In front of our building he called out my name, his voice approaching the register of a tweeter, and distorted into a thin, high-pitched wail. I cried and laughed, laying my head on his chest. He picked me up and pirouetted with joy, and I cried and laughed with even greater intensity. I understood for the first time what it meant to "weep with joy." My mother was quick to come down to put a stop to it. We went inside immediately. In college, I was able to see him only on weekends. I would wax eloquent about campus life and extracurricular activities, and suggested that he too joint the poetry club and the drama club, but his only interest was how to get a passing grade in the courses he took. In no time the Department of International Finance program at Jiaotong University transformed him into a glum-faced young man. He is now in Japan. He knows I have chosen writing as a career but is unaware that for a period of two years I could see the balcony of his parents' apartment from mine.

After picking up the keys for the apartment, I even hired a local feng shui expert to vet the place. I was able to announce to my boyfriend that the apartment had excellent feng shui and there was no danger of us breaking up (at least as long as we lived in that apartment), and that my writing career was full of promise. I didn't give any thought to how long we were going to stay there. Two months into our occupancy, some cardboard boxes of my belongings still remain unopened in my room. I swear I'll put the apartment in order as soon as I finish this novella. But my promises have long lost credibility with my boyfriend. That didn't stop me from making this latest vow. This novella shall not exceed forty thousand words. Therefore, the key is the choice of subject matter. Two days have gone by before you know it, and it is three days to the National Day, yet I still haven't written one single word. I went downstairs in the late afternoon. Kids of the apartment compound were going back and forth on their skates. Try taking a few steps, a mother rooted her daughter on. Why don't I try writing a grand narrative?

I can write about the Cultural Revolution, earthquakes, reform, floods, corruption.... I will have to amass a great amount of data first, and confront hard choices between those data sets. After the greater part of a year, with the cutoff date for submissions for the novella contest approaching, I would grow increasingly nervous, and the relationship with my boyfriend would suffer. I would shortly regain my serenity, telling myself those things were not worth being written into a novella. Naturally, it would be some time before I could forgive myself. If I produced a novella, I would have a chance at winning first prize and the award money of thirty thousand yuan. Then there is my mother, who has been looking forward to the day I receive an award. I never attended day care or kindergarten. On my fifth birthday, she gave me a dictionary of idiomatic expressions. When I realized I was expected to memorize a page of those expressions, I was speechless with shock. She wouldn't give me a break even on my birthday! That evening before bed, she opened the book to the first page and had me repeat the phrases from memory. Since I could remember only *ai wu ji wu* (he that loves the house, loves the crows on its roof) and *an bu dang che* (substitute walking for riding) from that page, she gave the palm of my hand a good spanking. I will never forget how she took me to Dong'an Park to play on the climbing net as part of her effort to teach me the art of essay writing. I'll be your playmate, she said. She stayed by my side and asked me to describe the image of the Monkey King at the top of the rope netting. It worked. I was soon hooked by this new game. When I was old enough to go to school, my favorite class was essay composition. I enjoyed filling in the blanks of the sheets of square checkered paper with strings of idiomatic expressions. You need to exercise restraint in using idiomatic expressions. You can use only one at a time. I am so grateful to my third grade language teacher for the advice.

What if I start to write a love story right away, complete it before the end of the year and become the first to submit it to the judges of the novella contest? Writing love stories is a straightforward thing: a brief description of how the two meet, followed as a matter of course by their tumbling into bed. One of them would carelessly throw away the love received from the other. Before age twenty-five, I did not realize that this was a way to keep you sane and sound physically and mentally. It works a little like the bloodletting technique in which a three-edged needle or a small, sharp knife is used to puncture the superficial meridians around the acupuncture points. Love, like *re du* (heat toxicity), a concept in traditional Chinese medicine, will suffocate you if some of it is not purged from the body. But I recall my mother's favorite mantra: You need to know both yourself and your enemy. I believe numerous contestants will write about love. The contest judges would sit in their comfortable chairs, drinking tea and chatting among themselves, and watch pile after pile of blazing flames quickly fizzle out and turn to ashes.

I was suddenly moved to Google the term "writing." Among the 15,500,000 results, the first returned was "World of Writing. Your Writing World. Write about Your World!" in large blue type followed by the line "The World of Writing is in the process of being restored …" in small black type. The first result returned by the Baidu search engine was "Writing for a living is no dream. The Tianxizhu Corporation will make your dream of becoming a writer come true!" I received my first writer's fee that came to all of fourteen yuan fifteen years ago. I am almost thirty now and I still don't own anything. My college mates and all my friends now own real estate. Even my mother does. But I still rent my place. I rarely go to dinner parties and make no new friends. Those columns I write exact a great deal of my energy although they have not yet exhausted it. I have to pull out all the stops to make them witty and interesting. All right, maybe I'm exaggerating. Let's click this link returned by Baidu and find out. The page opens to eight paragraphs. It's not until the last two paragraphs that the true message of the page dawns upon the reader. Is it necessary for me to recap those paragraphs? (It's enough that you know that the club offers large-storage email accounts for the paltry rent of one thousand yuan to clients who are interested in writing for a living). Under a list of account numbers, they make an enthusiastic pitch: Friend! Do you want to rewrite history? Then join now [Register for a Xintianzhong Club mailbox]! It will bring good fortune day after day and make your dream come true!

I dream almost every night. I have not had any dreams from which I wake up all excited. In fact I've never been bothered or unsettled by dreams. There was only that once, when I dreamed I lost a tooth on my left lower jaw. I sat up in my bed, believing that someone among my close kin was going to die. No sooner had it dawned the following morning than I phoned my mother, who was still drowsy and not yet fully alert, only to be told she was in very good health. My thought immediately turned to my biological parents and I was sure imminent death was stalking one of them. I don't know where they are now. I understand death comes to everybody. I only hope I can die in my own home. Perhaps my grandchildren would one day discover me in my bed, inert in my pajamas, and would only think I was asleep. If one can die in one's sleep, it's a sure sign that one had a former life remarkable for great virtue and charity. That's what my mother always says. I am sure I will one day die of vasospasm, beyond a shadow of a doubt. The headaches started already when I was fourteen. I hated it when my boyfriends touched my head. The back of my head was quite unsightly. It had the look of a bumpy road that had fallen into disrepair.

When the headaches came I didn't want to open my eyes. Sometimes they were accompanied by nausea. I would lay my head sideways on the pillow, to relieve the pressure on the side where pain was worst. I had a feeling that some blood vessel in my head was on the point of falling into small segments like a tired rubber band that had turned yellow and sticky. I imagined my cranium to be filled with blood that had no place to go and had a higher than normal temperature. My feverish thoughts flopped and thrashed about in my head, wading waist-high before being totally submerged. The moment the light in their eyes was extinguished, I seemed to see my soul rise up into the sky through a tunnel. I began to take pain killers, which I always carried around with me. I didn't want to have to run around in the street looking for a drugstore in an emergency. I was able to sleep again, but my memory deteriorated. The comforting thought is I got a break from my dear mother.

2

My former boyfriend asked me on MSN how I had been doing. We had not touched base for a long time.

I would never have thought that in the one year and four months since my former boyfriend left, I drew a complete blank in my writing history.

It was in March the year before last, three months after I got married. I was asked by a girlfriend of mine to meet her at a bar one evening. She'd boarded her cruise ship in Hong Kong and she had just finished her sightseeing in Putuo, Shanghai. With her were some editors, producers and directors, as well as an elderly man from Taiwan. They were having a great time talking among themselves. I should have stayed, out of courtesy, until ten and left the bar. Then nothing would have happened. But my dear girlfriend, who prided herself on being good at reading people's mind, had invited another friend of hers, just for my sake. He made his appearance and sat down in a chair next to me. To make a long story short, if I had not asked for his MSN address, we would not have chatted online so frequently. He was not a writer, but a music reviewer who had an unconventional writing style. Every evening I would sit at a desk placed behind my husband and chat with him. He started to speak about the new French novel. I was introduced for the first time to Jean-Philippe Toussaint and Christian Gailly. Doesn't he have to go to work tomorrow? My husband asked me. It was two or three in the morning when I finally shut down the computer. In order to dispel doubt from his mind, my husband invited him out to dinner. When my husband saw that he came accompanied by his girlfriend, his face spelled relief.

I wore a one-piece dress that totally covered bosom and back to meet him. The dress was loose-fitting and not equipped with a zipper. It was more like a sack. I did not wear a bra. The room was sweltering and he turned on the fan. He squatted before me and immediately seized my hand. He had a visible bulge. Our sexual impulse ran wild and we were naked in no time. It was time to go home, time to regain calm and control. But I was not interested in peaceful coexistence. I asked for a divorce. Some of my girlfriends found my decision rash and immature. Maybe I was immature, but I dislike telling lies. Marriage and home are no sacred cows to me. I remember the story of a girlfriend of mine. After she got married, another man with whom she had been madly in love for several years told her: I was worried that you would force me to divorce my wife. Now we are safe and we can be together again. She displayed her wedding portrait in a prominent spot on her office desk. I could not imagine having my body kissed and fondled by one man and passed on straight to another. He also told his young girlfriend he intended to leave her. He did his best to console his inconsolable friend. My divorce has been instrumental in my writing a book, which will be published next year. It will be available to readers in the not too distant future. As soon as the book is out, I will remind him to buy a copy. Alas, we had parted ways before I completed the book. I said to him: Go have fun! There's no need to come home early. I enjoy being alone. I could devote more time to writing. He did not come home one night. I had no idea where he spent the night and waited anxiously for his text message. The message finally came: Baby, I think I'm going to be naughty tonight.

I met the first boy with whom I wanted to be naughty with in my second year in high school (I would never have remembered him if I had not contemplated participating in the novella contest). He was a pen pal. He wrote to me saying that he had grown up in a hamlet by the Yellow River (I forget what his name was). He was then a student at the East China University of Science and Technology. I knew that he was highly regarded in his hamlet. One late summer afternoon, dressed in a crewneck sweater and white shorts, I succeeded in finding him. He immediately wanted to take me in his arms, but I decided to wait. By the end of the summer, I had lost interest. A friend of his wrote to inform me that after this blow the wretched boy lost several pounds (I couldn't imagine how he looked when he was reduced to a bag of bones). I wrote back: I decided not to continue the relationship merely because of too much schoolwork. Yes, it had nothing to do with his gawkiness or his constant heavy breathing through his nose. Why had I found his straight-to-the-point declarations of love and the way he clasped me in a tight embrace and caressed me crudely attractive? I shredded his letters in batches. When I was unsure what to do with the big teddy bear he gave me, my first love saw me holding the bear and came over to ask me what I was doing. I told him listlessly that I was disposing of some old stuff. I had a doll as big as this when I was a child, he said. The oversized doll was my surrogate for receiving spankings. When my mother wanted to warn me, she would hit it with a ruler until it became ragged. I believe his mother must have studied child psychology.

I could go on forever about my past romances. I wrote about some in other articles and I can continue writing about them. Writing about one's childhood is also relaxing. I spent a year to write a story with a profound message, at the risk of readers failing to get my point. Reviewers, like psychologists, want to get paid first before consenting to listen patiently to and analyzing what the authors wish to convey.

I was asked more than once by my boyfriend why I had chosen writing as a career. My reply was that I would feel miserable if I could not write (actually, the opposite is true, at least this time around. I've had several episodes of headache in the past few days). This was not true. But I didn't know how else to explain it. One day in a certain month of a certain year I found myself looking at a stack of newspapers. I was then writing advertising copy, charged with the task of touting the virtues of a number of things. For lack of better things to do that afternoon, I went out of my office and bought several newspapers for one yuan. It would take some time to read through the papers, and I would go home when the sun sank below the horizon. I sat at my desk and started reading. Parading before my eyes were alternating pages of flamboyant fashion, office politics and agonizing romances. Then all of a sudden a name, under the heading of an article, in a most obscure spot, buried in the unsexy sections, caught my eye. I was on the point of skipping that narrow column of text talking about a blue sky on a clear autumn day, when that name exercised a strange power over me and seized my attention. Zou Zou ("go, go" in Chinese), I said to myself, where does this author want to go?

Here I owe the reader an explanation: *zou* means running both in ancient Chinese and in modern Japanese. I enjoy running. I have frequent headaches, and after taking my pain killers I have a strong urge to crash into someone with a bang. Staggering in a world of psychedelic lights and shadows is a completely different sensation than when one is clear-headed. Some run in a comical manner, those of advanced age or laden with ungainly lard, the heels of their shoes tap-tapping on the pavement as if taking pleasure in misfortune of others, bravely running after a departed city bus. I also enjoy ambling aimlessly in the streets. High rises block the sun in the streets and alleys of the less prosperous neighborhoods, made colder by gusts of wind. Zou Zou, I could imagine how that person's arms swung in the act of writing. I stared at the name for a long while. What was I thinking at that moment? An obscure emotion prompted me to heave an exaggerated sigh, which caused some astonishment among colleagues sitting nearby, but they stayed at their desks. Then huge petals of an irrepressible joy burgeoned in my face. They saw it out of the corner of their eyes and started to scrutinize me with a quizzical look. I rose to my feet, waving the paper in my hand, but found the gesture inadequate to make them understand. I planted myself in front of the colleague closest to my desk and announced the good news (which nobody doubted).

I returned to my seat with my heart beating wildly. I reread the article: "I" described in that article how "I" climbed a mountain. It was a steep mountain with cable cars reaching its top, but "I" decided to climb it. "I" finally climbed to a great height, from where I commanded a view of the most beautiful scenery of the world. Mountain climbing is so boring; you get close to zero displacement for one thing, then there are those gnats and other bothersome flying insects that simply won't leave you alone. The plants are unremarkable. I could better satisfy my botanical curiosity in a botanical garden. Not to mention the ubiquitous eyesore of discarded plastic bottles and the patently false and contrived legends and vignettes about immortals gracing the various scenic spots. I should stuff the newspaper in a waste basket. When

I spread it open with both hands, that name hit my eyes again. Zou Zou! She is so perfect. She is the same age as I, has a soft, smooth complexion. She has the deep bass voice of a writer. She smokes, and keeps short fingernails to facilitate typing. I returned to my rented room at a near run. I found Zou Zou waiting for me. She came toward me, flustered and flushed. She began to tweak her looks, drawing her hair back into a neat ponytail. A black hair stuck out of her nostril. I yanked it out. The following day I had business cards made so that everywhere I went people would start using my new name.

I collected articles written by "Zou Zou" and would open my scrapbook after the day's work was over. I tried to love those articles as I loved that name. Unfortunately it didn't work. My interest waned. I had planned on having that person continue to write for me. I sent an article I had just finished to the editor of that same newspaper. But is that what happened? I can't be sure about the exact circumstances.

More than once though I discovered that Zou Zou was engaged in a trial of strength with me (it kept me on pins and needles). It appeared the other was on to my writing plan. No sooner had I written about my father and the column appeared in a magazine than I saw an article appear, written by that person, about that person's mother. I was planning to write about my mother after her passing. If my father had been alive, I would not have written one word about him. But someone had written about "My Mother." Not long ago I found a post on a literary website I frequently visit; it contained a novella I wrote. The person who posted it noted at the end of the article: This is a novella written by a "Zou Zou" I know. I just saw a work on another forum, also signed "Zou Zou." At first I thought it was the same person, but when I took a closer look I found it was not. Soon followed replies to the post: Of course it was not. The other "Zou Zou" doesn't write as well as this one. The third post went: Sigh, I know that, but did you have to be so direct? How come there is another Zou Zou here? The person who started the thread offered a rebuttal: This "Zou Zou" predates the other by a long shot, not just "another Zou Zou" as you said, my sister! I was sorely tempted to explain the genesis of my pen name but checked myself in time. This is not her fault, nor mine. Before the publication of my first novel, I found the mention of "woman writer Zou Zou" in Shi Kang's novel. She and "I" signed the contract and she poked a hand inside the male writer's clothes. Some of my friends were quite surprised, and sought clarification from me. I told them it was a pure coincidence. I considered it par for the course that several Zou Zous were writing at the same time. I am indebted no end to that "Zou Zou." Of course my becoming a writer has been preordained in my karma; all "Zou Zou" did was accidentally flicking a switch. From that day on, everything else in my world fell into darkness, except for one thing that shone brightly and persistently: a yearning, in its myriad, dazzling variations, to tell a story, which would have an unshakable claim on me for the rest of my life, I thought.

When I was a kid, my mother often wondered what I could do when I grew up. As she saw it, a teaching job at some magnet middle school would be nice. Being among young people will rejuvenate you, and you'll not end up being forgotten by people. An engineer of the human soul! What a noble sounding profession! My mother wanted an ordinary, happy life for me. Despite my outward indistinguishability with the other kids in our little alley, I knew I was a precious jade hidden in an ordinary looking stone. Only, not many people have the Wisdom Eye to spot hidden talent. My mind keeps wandering back to that lady editor who worked for a best-selling magazine but whose conversation was dull and boring. Why weren't any questions raised about her qualifications? I was young then, a college kid. I went to see this old editor working for a literary magazine targeting young people, to listen to her comments on my virgin work. The spiral staircase was wide enough for two abreast, but it was deserted and I heard only my own footsteps. I found her by following bursts of laughter behind a door. She began with some praise, which was immediately followed by a stream of words that signified cold rejection, which was the real point she wanted to convey. Now whenever there is a change in the weather, as, for instance, when I boarded a boat to Taohua (Peach Blossom) Island in bright sunshine only to be met with pouring rain the moment I stepped off the boat, I would think of her. She said those words gingerly, carefully weighing them, and bowed her head after saying them. She rubbed her eyes with her hands, as if to show she felt worse than I. Very well, she finally let her hands fall back to her side, continue writing. Write only what you want to write, young lady. On my way home I walked into that little bookstore once again, and as usual, I flipped through pages rapidly, scanning the lines as fast as I could, my fingers only pausing at pithy paragraphs to silently memorize them. But this time the suction cups of my memory failed and I turned and walked out of the store.

Those beautiful sheets of manuscript paper of mine now lay fallow. When I went home on Saturday, my mother had as usual prepared a meal for me. No, I don't eat ginger! I screamed at her as she brought me the bowl of soup, the meatballs sprinkled with diced yellow ginger bobbing in the bowl in rhythm with the slow shuffling of her feet. What have you written lately? Her tone was cheerful. I replied by chewing noisily. This routine lasted until I found an internship in an ad agency. I did my best to make my job of copy writing sound interesting, and soon my mother forgot my dream to become a writer. But that dream started to glow, in its own good time, of its own free will, as I lay alone on my cool mat, surrounded by darkness.

A few months later I brought that newspaper home. My mother shot a glance at me, and retrieved her reading glasses from the drawer of the sewing machine. She started reading it, and then read it a second time, and a third time. A flush rose in my face. Why did you pick the name "Zou Zou"? She turned the paper over to look at the other page. After a while she picked up the thread again: The name sucks! It will bring bad luck. Things would run, run away. Why don't you change it to "Lai Lai" (Come Come)? No, I like Zou Zou, I told her. The following day I found that little newspaper column showcased under a glass top polished to a shine. The excitement of the moment over, I knew that from this moment on I'd have to prove my worth under that name.

It all started like this. I clipped the articles written by "Zou Zou" from the newspapers that carried them, and carefully studied their beginnings, evolutions, denouements and endings. It took one day to piece together a brand new story from among them. She must have small hands like mine. She would sit very still at her desk, her eyes riveted on the computer monitor, and I would be present at all times, eagerly waiting for line after line to appear in the Word document. Sometimes she would be unable to produce a single word for a long span, and I would share her anguish and torment at such moments. It didn't take long before I decided to allow a photo of myself to appear in a small newspaper. I've preserved that issue in my collection. The picture was small and blurry. It was taken by my boyfriend of the time. It showed me hunched before a computer, my hair covering completely my forehead and my face slighted turned up, and my eyes radiating a fine intelligence dogged by a certain melancholy.

I was pleased for a while after seeing the picture published, and decided to pay a visit to that old friend of mine. She embedded a lot of information in her writings, so I knew where to find her. I found the building. A light rain forced me to seek shelter in the corridor. I knew her home was behind that door in my back. I waited a long time, pressing the bell several times without getting any response. I left without seeing her. I went home after spending some time window shopping. In the hallway I ran into my mother, who was on the point of unlocking the door. She was carrying a red sponsored umbrella under her arm and holding in her hand a paper bag of fried *shengjian* dumplings.

From that day on, I became a bona fide, full-fledged woman writer. I bought a membership at a beauty spa, spending a lot of time lying on a white couch and being fussed over, surrounded by the sound of Mazak and hatching one inspiration after another like a hen laying eggs. I strolled alongside the flower beds on paths paved with crushed stones, a pensive expression on my face. I recognized none of the plants in the flower beds. Those old coots walked by me in their socks, having eyes only for the crushed stones that promised better health. I intended to buy a nice paper weight at the Liuli Crystal Workshop to ornament my simple desk. They were charging an outrageous price of seven hundred yuan for that piece of glass! I sighed ruefully. Why did I become a writer? I believe a wry smile must have flicked across my face. The salesgirl shrieked: You are a writer?

3

It's time I start writing. It's Friday, November 3. I plan to write a novella whose heroine is a photogenic young woman writer (it's always easier to write about a writer than about some cursed hitman), who is driven by the characters populating her head to produce one lyrical story after another. She retreats to a room with four bare walls and a desk and not much else. She has a computer, but she can't resist the temptation to browse the shopping site Taobao, to look at those lovely dresses, shoes and handbags (I have to say this for her: she needs an occasional change of scene. It helps her writing). Her masterful use of idiomatic expressions shows her at her most creative. Her writing is peppered with them. Those idiomatic expressions seem to have taken on a life of their own and to have learned to self-propagate, and it's only after a life-and-death struggle with them that she manages to pare them down to produce a crisp, spare prose. You sit up all night day after day in this room. What is it you are doing? Her boyfriend says with a nagging suspicion. She opens all her email accounts and searches the inboxes for love letters dating back five years and rereads them. Some of the love letters were used in books she wrote. On days when the sky is a clear blue, she would occasionally go out. Once she was heading for the park and was passing a street vendor who was selling chestnuts roasting on an open fire, when she was seized with self-reproach. I have to go back to work (Yes, the park can be visited anytime. I should finish the novel first. There will be plenty of time to visit it then). So she returned to her desk. Of course I will allow her to sleep. The poor girl suffers migraines from time to time that can only be relieved by taking four pill tablets at a time. While she waits for the drug to take full effect, she will be allowed to lie down, and watch a DVD, or maybe practice some yoga? That would improve her health.

The idea hit me with a sudden, powerful force. I was lying at the side of my boyfriend, who, as usual, wrapped himself tightly in his blanket and was sweating profusely. I walked barefoot into the living room, and poured myself a glass of water. The room was flooded by bright sunshine. I noticed a box of pineapple slices on the dining table, half of which had been consumed, while the remaining slices had browned slightly at the edges. I poured some all-natural, health-enhancing birch syrup into my glass, and observed with satisfaction the pallor and anemic look of my hands in the sunlight. The jarring notes of the violin seeped in again from the hallway. All of this conspired to create a sense of disorientation in my fragile and sensitive being, which, under the glare of the sun, slowly receded to give way to a mist of wistfulness. I found my comfort and contentment in the mist. I woke up to the voice of my boyfriend, who said, looking at me: Hey, why are you lying on the floor? I told him that the ideas for my story galloped at such a speed I totally forgot where I was. To prove this, I turned on my black laptop right away. The image of the heroine Zou Zou was bright and clear, like the sunlight blazing through the window. She walked toward me, with a kind of saunter as if she hadn't a care in the world. She looked about her, appearing to examine her surroundings attentively (women are naturally drawn to store windows, ergo the need for women writers like me with the fertility of our imagination, and our unique verbal and rhetorical skills). She wore a wrinkled, floor-length hemp cloth robe, the color of which was, naturally, black, because black symbolized mystery (in the eyes of women writers, wrinkles are synonymous no doubt with elegance and hemp cloth is testament to the rebelliousness of a princess who has run away from her palace). Sometimes lines of text would fly across the screen, at other times there were long pauses when she ruminated. The man who was totally devoted to her didn't know what to do faced with her serious mien, but in the next moment, she swung gently around to face him and started to dance barefoot on his feet (should she write about that man's poor dance skills?). My boyfriend identified a problem. He said: Don't you realize your portrayal of the writer was stereotyped? Of course I did! I told him I preferred to portray this writer as one that fitted the readers' perception of writers. I did not set out to do a faithful portrayal of her true self. Let her speak for herself! My boyfriend patted me on my shoulder. How do I make her speak for herself? By paying her?

Slipping an envelope stuffed with cash on her desk when she dozed off in front of her computer? Do I deduct the income tax before paying her fee? Maybe you should pay her a visit first.

Her computer was on. The keyboard (black keys with white letters) lay inert under the blue glare of the monitor. I felt as if the keyboard was staring at me. She died young. Sitting before her computer, she was going to type in the last line of her work when a blood vessel burst and she died quietly. Her last, unfinished work left the literary world in nail-biting suspense. It soon spread like a wild fire. Her posthumous fame grew tremendously. On a day set aside to honor her memory an award was set up to challenge people to carry on her legacy, with first prize fetching thirty thousand yuan.... Sigh! My train of thought is always disrupted by my inspirations. But I am happy with the idea. I was going to reconstruct her brief but brilliant life in reverse chronology, when I was surprised by her voice. Let me cook supper this evening. You will love spaghetti with buttered tuna. Picking up her handbag from the sofa, she said: I'm going to get some groceries. I'll go with you, said the man on the sofa, as he got up, held out his pale hairy hand and took her by her waist.

I thought they would be back shortly, but more than two hours would elapse before they finally returned. I almost lost my patience. She could have written at least two thousand words in that time interval! It was distressing. She was squandering away her time. She put on an apron to go into the kitchen, as the man (I have come to deeply resent him, despite his good looks) started to play a video game. But I tried hard to calm myself down. The yoga deep breathing technique really helped. I told myself she was experiencing life and when she resumed writing she would write much better than when she was alone (this is indispensable for women writers).

But I would be proved wrong, very wrong. A month later, I found that she was going out more frequently. She would disappear on weekends together with that man. Men are truly the stumbling block to women's progress, especially women who are writers. Men invade their space, and continuously nibble away at their free time for creative work. In the beginning it feels like a fish bone stuck in your throat, but you get used to it after a while (what can't humans get used to?). Of course every woman writer inevitably mentions men in every novel she writes. Even if she is still a virgin or well past menopause, she will inevitably have men around her for some length of time, but eventually she has to shake them off. If they always have men on top of them, they will cease to exist. As for house work, nothing could be worse than that! Most women writers solve that dilemma by hiring a live-in nanny, or at a minimum an hourly one, to take care of their housekeeping. How can I be so callous as to have a beautiful woman writer do her own dishes, and pots and pans, and allow all that grease to clog the intricate networks of her brain, like it chokes up the sewers? Right now she looks not much different from what she was before, maybe even somewhat cheerier and better dressed. But she is living with that man, that's a fact. It is impossible to circumvent him. So how does one go about stopping his intrusions? I paid her a visit when she was alone and had a talk with her. I told her that writing was purely her own business. That man's only use for her was helping her maintain glandular wellbeing. She sat up abruptly in her bed and made her way to the bathroom. A sticky stuff trickled down from her groin, sullying every inspiration of mine! I charged at her, unsteadily and in anger. Calm down, she said, looking at me out of the corner of her eyes, her voice lowered to a whisper, he can provide memory, lots of memories, which I need. All you have to do is pick and choose, and weave them into the novel, bit by bit, painstakingly.

I am ready to be patient. Sometimes I feel this novella is already a finished work. I can clearly visualize it in a magazine: black fine type in two or three columns and a check for thirty thousand yuan handed to me amid looks of curiosity and respect. I express my thanks absent-mindedly, rubbing the check between my fingers (it's not as crisp as a brand new hundred-yuan bill). The heady experience of being interviewed by the media. My mother's happy smile. I invited some friends for tea and dinner, and give them a passionate, detailed talk about this "insignificant thing." One autumn day, about two years ago, one of them had given me some source material concerning the transformation of a hamlet. I told him that I'd been working with the story he gave me for two years, but I had to finish this work first. He appeared pleased and told me more stories. Wonderful! I have to write them down (I know I can't use them, so I have to be doubly careful with them). I threw in some imaginary details, and as I did so I was quite impressed with myself as a writer. It's a good thing you have started to write again, he said. Yes, I nodded animatedly. And so another month went by.

My mother said to me: It's three years since you last published a novel. You will soon be forgotten. Oh dear Mama, I don't think those teachers of mine will ever forget me. On Teachers' Day, I paid my old high school a visit. Most of those teachers were still working there. The gym teacher still vividly remembered the time I made in the eight-hundred-meter dash. You always walked into the school at the exact moment the bell rang for class. The physics teacher said the article I wrote about him was a fine piece of work. I'm glad I confiscated it at the time. I still have it. But I did not grant him the copyright to it. Evidently the very first time they clapped eyes on me, they already sensed there was something in me that made me stand out from the rest of the crowd. The time has come for this specialness to realize its true and full value. A writer, a great writer, will unabashedly insert her thin silhouette into the fat annals of literature.

Put aside your novel for the moment and let's travel. My boyfriend gave me a peck on the forehead. In his eyes, writing is not merely a noble pastime, but an art. In France, you have to have an encyclopedic knowledge and solid self-confidence before you dare to pick up the pen. They are inspired by angels, he said, this is precisely why I am deeply attracted to you. He teaches at the Alliance Française. To reach the institute you walk up three floors receiving little natural light (a continuing education college is housed on those floors with dirty tiles). But on the fourth floor, there is plenty of sunlight. The small classrooms on that floor are furnished with soft wallpaper of a dark blue color. He walked with a steady gait into the room, the perennial serious expression on his face lit up by two sparkling eyes. He gave out his MSN address to the class. Every evening after supper we would chat online late into the night. Sometimes I would capture his eyes and lips through the ether. Now these words that just issued from his thin lips were so enticing. I've been cooped up in this small room since the end of summer, whose windows I rarely opened because noise hurts my fragile nerves more than stale air. We last traveled to the Putuo Mountains. We rode in a fast boat together a few times. The vegetation was lush, the beer tasted like lukewarm drinking water. Not long after our arrival, it began to rain steadily and our shoes were caked with mud. The trip cost a pretty penny, but I have not regretted it. On a trip before that one, we went up a big mountain infrequently visited by tourists. There we found only one small restaurant, which offered very bland fare. On the third day, I began to miss the pastries in the cafés of Shanghai. The only structures of note were a square and a bronze horse. Before every trip I always prepare a detailed checklist: changes of underwear, skin care items, razors to shave the armpits, and sometimes a bottle of mineral water. All right, let's take a trip. This time we chose a seaside town. A friendly town surrounded by blue, according to the web site.

That town proved no different from others. Cab fare was somewhat cheaper. The lighting in cafés was just as dim. At the center of the town square stood a big, symmetrical flower garden, and a fountain was, naturally, de rigueur. People were dressed casually, and paid scant attention to my outfit, which was the result of elaborate preparation and fussing on my part every morning. There is nothing new under the sun, I quoted from the Bible, but my boyfriend was busy looking around him. Look at that owner! He is panting with his mouth wide open only because he is obese. And look at that one. I think she is going to light up a cigarette now. I followed the direction of his eyes and saw an entirely mundane scene, with people nattering, their mouths opening and closing. Somewhat discouraged, I scrutinized my boyfriend with fresh eyes. This seemingly cheerful guy was practicing his awkward Chinese. I turned up the collar of my sweater and subsided once again into a mournful, much needed silence.

The following morning I spread out the tourist map. The points of interest, in dense clusters, were marked on the map. Let's go, I said, let's visit these places. But my boyfriend responded by shifting heavily in the bed. So I had to set off without him. I did feel much better once I got close to the sea. The water was not blue but neither was it too murky. I went for a leisurely walk on the sand, glad that I had remembered to put on my sunscreen, but no sooner had the thought entered my head before I gave it a shake. Perish the vulgar thought! It is unworthy of a woman writer to commune with nature. I merely shook my hair and passed my hand over it, and lo and behold, a woman's face popped up, a smiling face, appearing I don't know from where, so suddenly that I was caught off guard and startled in no small measure. But when I took a closer look, the fear receded. This face looked so familiar to me. She started to smile and talk to me. Her voice also sounded familiar, as though it had always resided in my ears, and had showed its true self only today. What's going through your mind? Tell me. She asked repeatedly. I sat down on the sand (again an inner voice told me I should sit with my back to the sun) and began to search my vocabulary. The ocean is an inexhaustible fountain of beer. There is always another glass of it. This is not a very elegant sentence. It's not as good as what you used to think up. What right does she have to judge? I was annoyed. I am but an unfitting transient that is accidentally mirrored with astounding clarity in the eyes of a boy. Where did you see him? I wanted very much to get to the bottom of who owned this face, but at the same time I was trying hard to visualize what I could give her. I saw him at a nameless spot by the sea, diagonally opposite me, on a rocky outcrop. I was standing as the light was failing, and he wore a bright outfit. What did you wear? A black sweater that left the neck visible. I did not wear makeup, so I did not look glamorous (But you must know that cosmetics are used to fool those puerile souls), but that was precisely why he was approaching me. Were you meeting him for the first time? I may have done so on an earlier day, in some garden, by a table, onto which a rain of cherry blossom petals was falling, when branches were swaying and my long hair hung low. Didn't you exchange any words? I was progressively less bothered by this strange face and was drawn deeper into the narrative of my story. No, I was talking to my boyfriend, but I smiled to him. In a sense, one might say we spent that afternoon together. Oh how eager I was to touch his face in order to be able to tell myself he was real, flesh and blood. What will you say to him this time by the sea? I'll talk about everything from my childhood, up to yesterday when we checked into the seaside hotel. What will the two of you do after that? He said: I'll take you to my room. He walked ahead of me in long strides. He pushed his door open. And the bed started creaking. Not that again! The face cried impatiently. Her voice became hoarse when she got agitated. Let me think, yes, I followed him, with my head bowed. When I lifted up my head again, I found myself alone. Where did he go? I didn't know. I started to look for him. When I was so exhausted in my search I couldn't even lift my feet, I found myself back in that same garden, and he was sitting on a bench under the trees, with a girl in his arms. They looked at me with curious eyes. All of a sudden I heard a peal of laughter behind me. I turned around to find my boyfriend standing at my back, in great merriment, shaking with laughter. His face appeared chubby and bright from good sleep. Very good, write it down. With that the face vanished and I was relieved, although I couldn't help going over the story I had told her once more in my mind. A kid holding a balloon tied to his finger with a string ran past me. I was feeling the heat of the sun.

I had a suspicion that the face was lurking in my hair, so I decided I would not touch my hair, but my boyfriend said my hair was disheveled and dirty. I washed and scrubbed it vigorously, but she did not reappear. When I combed my hair after rinsing it, she still did not appear. I marveled at how easy it was to get rid of her, and I went out to dinner. The next morning I went to the seaside again, fully expecting her to surprise me with her reappearance, but she did not. We returned to Shanghai that evening.

4

My life returned to its rut, to business as usual, holding no surprises. I attended an exhibition this evening, where a friend told me I looked a bit plump. When he uttered the word "plump," I immediately visualized a short, fat, haggard-looking woman wearing a pair of boots that was last year's fashion. I told him this lady he was looking at had been ruined by the ruthless stress of writing. As I elaborated on that statement, I nudged my way to the long table covered with party food, and went on to sample every kind of canapé I could get my hand on. When I pushed my way through the crowd away from the table, I spotted Zou Zou, who held a bottle of beer in her hand, not far from where I was (I believe she deliberately chose to keep a safe distance from me). I really couldn't stand the way she had her eyes boring into you. I too looked at her fixedly, and to my surprise she responded with a child-like smile. I turned and walked out of the exhibition hall, and she followed. When I wheeled around abruptly, she also stopped and gave me a toothy grin. What do you want from me? I demanded in a whisper as I walked toward her. Where is she? A lightning pain shot across my left brain and I moaned, seizing my head with my hands. All she wanted was to take back her name, wasn't it? With my hands holding one side of my head, I looked all over for her but couldn't find her. It began to rain in the street.

I took a taxi home and when I found my boyfriend lying on the sofa watching TV, I burst out crying. What's the matter? He sat up and took me in his arms, the copper button on his sleeve cuff feeling cold against my cheek. Minutes later I was blowing my nose into a tissue. Between the mist of tears and the white tissue I saw a black dress making its way toward me. She plunked herself down at my side, and started to cry quietly with her hands covering her face. After a while she reached across the coffee table and fumbled for a tissue. I have a headache, I said to my boyfriend in a coquettish voice and nimbly maneuvered myself onto his lap, making sure to leave no gap between him and me. He uncoiled my top knot bun, and started to give me a massage. She wiped her eyes, nose and mouth soundlessly, her body reclining on the other end of the sofa, and her eyes staring fixedly at me.

I am perfectly aware now that no matter what dress she is in, she is Zou Zou. And once she has come into my life, there is no getting rid of her again, just as those big buttocks of hers are now firmly and resolutely glued to my sofa. I didn't want my boyfriend to see her. Who knows but that she would snatch him from me? She would follow me into my household, sit under that bonsai tree of good fortune and eat the chocolate on my table. She would sniff at the fragrant rosemary plant by the sofa and suddenly get up to fetch a carton of milk past its expiration date from the fridge and pour all of it on the plant. She complained about the persistent heavy fogs of this winter and the not very user-friendly remote of the air conditioner. My boyfriend would either continue to stoically play his SimCity games, or wear an astonished look. That's enough! I can't stand it any longer! But she stood up at this moment, that familiar pensive expression creeping into her face, and she crossed to the computer. She opened the Word document entitled *Writing*, and proceeded to tap on the keyboard, as if she had never left it.

When I looked in on her the next morning, she was still sitting there, her hands on the keyboard, but her expression had changed to a worried frown. Cigarette butts of varying lengths lay in the ashtray at her right. In my attempt to read what she had written, I startled her. She smiled and threw a naughty wink at me. Well, how did the writing go? I asked. You will find out in due time, she said, there are several scenarios. She drew up her chair toward me, and that unsettled me a little. She held both my hands in hers and put her head on my lap. After the completion of this novel, let's quit writing, all right? Why? I asked. No reason, she said, I just feel that would be better. You shouldn't be here, I said, you've disrupted my life. I've done nothing of the sort, she retorted.

Of course, my life goes on. My poor boyfriend has finally understood that I am inseparable from this computer in front of me. He could not know that those sessions in front of the computer were actually tête-à-têtes between Zou Zou and me. Sometimes it was a knee-to-knee chat between us. I was more and more intrigued by the look in her eyes, which always expressed something whose meaning I could not fully fathom. But I was also well aware of the danger she posed, so much so that I decided to overcome my own social inadaptability and try to keep her at my side as much as possible. I did this partly to be able to monitor her writing progress up close, but more importantly, to dispel my suspicion of her on the many occasions when my boyfriend would mysteriously disappear for a couple of hours.

I just can't wrap my head around the profession of "writing." Don't you find yourself mediocre? What can you do besides writing? You have no real skills. Being a mediocre writer is quite pointless. These comments by Zou Zou only showed how crafty she was. To me writing is purely for my own amusement, a hobby, and occasionally a source of some modest income. But her criticism was vicious. Doesn't she know I enjoy some name recognition in certain circles? I showed her the latest issue of Oggi for the Chinese market, in which an ad for Dove chocolates featured me with my bony little face cocked slightly to one side. Then tell me what is more worth doing? Living! Zou Zou answered. Your writing suffers because you are not interested in living. You can't blame it on anyone else. But I have fame. My fame is a full vindication of the worth of my writing. Let's face it. You are just jealous of me.

I was never truly mad at her. In rare sunny winter days, we sauntered along the tactile paving strips for the blind on the sidewalk. Negotiating the "tactile sidewalk strips" helps you gain a true understanding of the act of walking, Zou Zou declared. I move forward along the tactile paving with my eyes shut and imagine whether I would crash into someone. The tactile paving lanes inspire a sense of suspense. True, every suspenseful step taken was uncomfortable and I privately grudged every such step. Although the soles of my boots were not as thick as I would have liked, I often managed to walk in great strides and leave her far back. I could imagine how she pressed her lips tightly together. Every time I went out with my boyfriend, I would press my lips together for a good few minutes before shouting out: Can you slow down a bit? He would immediately turn around and take out a cigarette.

After every walk, I would ask Zou Zou: Have you got any new ideas? I am sure you have got some bright ones now. But she would sigh and say: Ah, how can you be so impatient? But I was so convinced that taking walks would benefit our writing career that I changed my MSN name to "On the Road, Bubbling with Writing Ideas." An interesting reaction to the name change came three days later. One net friend thought I had switched to writing smartphone novels. He said he was worried because writing with one's thumbs on a device could be so absorbing that doing it while walking constituted a traffic hazard.

You look tired, my boyfriend said, as he poured some tomato meat sauce onto my white plate. It is said that ten or more teaspoons of tomato sauce a week helps slow down aging. As the tart red sauce passed over my tongue, I imagined an instant effect on my wrinkles. That's enough! Enough! I moved the plate away when my boyfriend tried to pour more sauce onto it. A drop of the stuff containing active ingredients possessing potent anti-oxidant properties fell on the table, missing its chance to perform wonders. You look too tired. Sitting for long hours every day in front of the computer is surely bad for your health. See, your buttocks have grown bigger again. This is only a novella, I said. But you think about it even in sleep. I heard you talk in your sleep yesterday. You can't go on like this. You must relax more. We need to make love. I gazed at him without seeing. Zou Zou did not budge on the sofa. You finally shaved today. But not close enough here, on your chin. I scrutinized him closely. He just had a haircut and his sideburns were trimmed very short. A small ridge was formed at the top with styling mousse. I share your feeling, but night time is my most productive period of the day when I am bursting with ideas, which I don't intend to interrupt. My boyfriend picked up a book without saying a word more and, squeezing through the narrow gap between me and the coffee table, left the room. I watched him disappear behind the bedroom door, and gave Zou Zou a quick nod. We returned together to the computer.

Progressing at the rate of one thousand words a day, we have now written almost eighteen thousand words. Although it still falls far short of the target of forty thousand, this hand-crafted little boat is beginning to take shape. Due to the crudeness of its present state of construction, it appeared to roll and pitch in an ocean heaving with an uncertain ending and teeming with ambiguities. I couldn't will myself to ignore these ambiguities and uncertainties. I lay in bed feeling very sleepy. Sleep was spreading slowly like a cobalt blue night sky, poised to cast a pall over every inch of me, but the ambiguities and uncertainties slid under the shroud to dangle at close range in front of my eyes. They gradually came into focus to produce a big bright moon. Another examination with sober eyes was warranted. Does it suffer from a certain levity? (Levity will give the work as a whole a flimsy feel) Does it lack intellectual depth? (Although, to take the analogy of the vitamin C in apples, an orchard farmer would hardly give any thought to the vitamin as he plants an apple tree. Nor will an apple eater give any thought to it as he bites into the fruit) Are there other possibilities for describing the experiences of the characters in the story? (There is the compatibility between those experiences and the personalities of the characters to consider) When day broke, I began to feel the subtle onset of a headache. I couldn't pinpoint the specific location. It must be because dissatisfaction with some parts of the writing was trapped in my head. I went to Zou Zou for help, hoping that she could ameliorate them and find an exit for my dissatisfaction. But it is like eating a pancake. You never succeed in chewing it into a neat, symmetrical shape. No sooner is one door opened than another locked door pops up. Besides, I overestimated her executory ability, believing that she would be able to render the desired effect faithfully. When I told her one morning that there was an overabundance of detail and not enough plot, she lit up a cigarette before embarking on a long lecture, even asserting that success depended on details. She went on to encourage me to make a bold attempt at "narrative adventure." Novels are no longer narratives of adventures, do you understand? I shrugged in a noncommittal way. I discerned on her face a subtle glow that only someone as keen on observing life as I could have detected. I understand, I said, but you must rein in your own enthusiasm and preferences. You know very well that we are doing this to get the prize. I became animated and began a diatribe on the importance of the thirty thousand yuan prize to me.

I am quite hard up now, I said. Thirty thousand yuan means two thousand five hundred yuan a month. I am paid two thousand a month by the publisher of the magazine I work for. I dare say you have never met a rich man, she cut me off unceremoniously, go find yourself a rich man! Then you won't need to draft me to ghostwrite your novels. Admit it! You want to enjoy the good life as much as everyone else. Don't try to corrupt me! You think all women writers would stoop to that, especially one as pretty as I, am I correct? Every pretty woman writer has an unlikely lover behind her, she sighed, looking me up and down with a frown. She reached out to touch my skin with her fingers but quickly drew back. You need to take better care of yourself. Who are you after all? I don't know you at all. Me? I am fine. I have never had any serious health problems. I had a persistent cough when I was a child, she said, and I suffer from mild arthritis. I didn't mean that, I cut her off impatiently, I meant, isn't writing a serious business? I consider myself a serious writer. You see, I have never written for soap operas. A fortune teller told me that I will have a good life before age 35, but my old age, alas, will be miserable, she said in an indifferent, even tone. Now listen carefully! I am talking to you about this coming contest, which is very important to me. You too need money, I know it. Why else are you making yourself a permanent guest in my home? Let's work hard for the prize, and I'll let you have half of the money. You'll be able to go out in pretty dresses and find a new boyfriend. I find our collaboration quite ridiculous. She turned away.

From that day on I tried not to be alone with her in the same room. I spent most of the day in the living room, where there was ample sunlight, which described lines and shapes on the bright wooden floor. But I did not fail to notice, with satisfaction, that she was looking more and more haggard, with big, dark circles under her eyes, and proliferating pimples on her face. One day she told me she had swollen gums. Poor Zou Zou! The thought that all these proved that she had given her all to the project elated me. I insisted that she should rest more, but I was getting impatient in the wait for the grand finale of the novella.

One weekend evening a girlfriend of mine invited me to a hot pot dinner. She introduced me as a famous writer to all her friends, and attempted at explaining why it was best not to mention pretty woman and writer in the same breath. This was not difficult, for they were unanimous in considering me a pretty woman. But soon, very soon, a loquacious central figure made his appearance. It was a middle-aged man with indifferent looks, who had an unshakable conviction that his former title of associate editor obligated him to maintain the noise level above 60 decibels in the room. As his petite wife looked meekly at him, an expression of ineffable happiness lit up her face. She moved her fingers a few times so that the ring "costing tens of thousands of yuan" on one of her fingers gave off a few timid, restrained glints. She was not pretty, and kept turning her head in different directions, in the belief that by this casual gesture she was making her vaunted dimpled beauty visible to all, although there was no depth to her dimples. My girlfriend was the first to spot the necklace I was wearing and deduce that I did not like the ones she had given me. Why aren't you wearing them? I blame myself for thinking I understood you.

Ah, that man was despicable! I don't recall who disdainfully broached the subject. The story started with his popularity as a poet in college. When a girl who had never been in love before appeared on the scene, the story headed toward tragedy, a tragedy of a virgin deceived by a married man. A friend was quick to "kick a dog when it's down." It is symptomatic of a problem for a girl in her twenties not to have experienced love. Someone interrupted her immediately. What was most unfortunate was the ex-virgin got pregnant. My girlfriend uncharitably called that poet a slug. Only the former associate editor put up a passionate defense for that absent poet, thrice emphasizing that his decision to recruit that man was based solely on his talent regardless of his past, and that the best generals are good at looking at the big picture, as he did.

After the subject was exhausted, those friends started to form groups in defiance of the distances across the big round table. As I struggled quietly with a piece of enoki mushroom lodged between my teeth, a lady sitting diagonally across the table from me told me with an envious expression that I had such a fine complexion. Could her eyes really penetrate the layers of makeup and skin care products applied on my face to detect the state of my complexion? But the tip of my tongue proved powerless to triumph over the entrenched enoki mushroom.

Finally, around ten thirty in the evening I

returned to my own apartment. What was happening there caught me wide-eyed and open-mouthed. Zou Zou was sitting on my boyfriend's lap. Give me a kiss, she said in French, laughing, a man asked me to go to a movie with him tonight but I refused. He really gave her a kiss! Dudu! I exclaimed, Dudu, what are you doing?

What's the matter with you? The smile was gone from my boyfriend's face. Why are you yelling? He asked in a gentle voice with a quizzical look on his face. Look at what you are doing! And you! Your seat is not here. It is in the other room. You are supposed to sit in front of the computer. If you don't get up this minute, I'm going to make you! Zou Zou stood up meekly, wiggled her waist and buttocks before hauling her big ass back to its rightful place. Tell me! When will that novella be completed? I asked her. How many more words before you're done? Twenty thousand words, she replied.

You are so pretty today! I forgot to tell you that before you left the apartment, my boyfriend said as he followed me into the bedroom. But, I said as I took off my earrings, I don't feel well. I am not well at all, I told him miserably. Then let's go to bed early, he said quickly, dropping the hands he had laid on my shoulders. Go take a shower while I prepare the bed and turn on the electric blanket for you. No, I'm not up to taking a shower, I'm too tired. You don't mind if I skip the shower for one night, do you? Does that mean we will not be able to make love again tonight? This is not good. Every Frenchman will agree with me that one's sex life is very important. Why are you feeling unwell again? Did you eat something that didn't agree with you or do you not love me anymore? You have me worried.

It will all go away soon, all, I promise, I murmured, resting my head on his chest. You are too tired, my poor little thing! Are you sure you want to continue writing? Tomorrow I'll be half way through. On the whole I don't write half so badly. You'll see the prize money. He smiled, tilting up my little head, the mysterious, complicated little head of a literary genius, and bestowing a kiss on it.

In a short while, I allowed my boyfriend to think that I'd fallen asleep. He was considering if he should turn off the desk lamp, finally deciding to angle the lampshade toward the base of the wall. He tiptoed out and noiselessly closed the door after him. I lay in bed, feeling very uncomfortable in my pajamas. For a fleeting moment I was seized by a paranoid vision of my boyfriend joining Zou Zou and the thought sent a swift arrow of pain through my heart. I listened intently for any sound or movement outside the door, and even sat half way up, when the door knob turned slowly and my boyfriend walked in. He felt my face and placed a kiss on the mouth that had gone to sleep. I knew that those were soft, warm lips. He tried not to touch my head as he walked around to the other side of the bed to take his pillow with him. Then he once again tiptoed out of the bedroom. Shortly after that I fell asleep, this time for real.

I woke up with a start, because my body felt a change. Coldness compelled me to curl up for warmth. I took one hand from under the cover despite the freezing cold to discover that I still had two blankets on me. I adjusted the temperature setting of the electric blanket to "high," but the cold refused to let go of me. Meanwhile, lumps of dough were being kneaded in my head by an invisible hand into unpredictable shapes. I was aware of a moaning through my nose. The door knob turned slowly.

I saw my boyfriend sitting down by the bed, and

inserting awkwardly a thermometer into my mouth. Zou Zou hid behind him, her body shielded by his sleeveless black down jacket. The sight of the two of them unabashedly appearing together set off a few angry moans from me. Those lumps of dough were growing bigger and heavier. I had to force myself to remain sober, and I could only accomplish that by breathing heavily. I'll get some medicine for you at the drugstore. With that my boyfriend was gone.

Zou Zou, why don't you leave? I finally said it! Only a short time ago, before the invasion of the coldness, I had a pleasant dream. I was an average hardworking white collar employee at an ad agency. I went straight home after work. My boyfriend and I sat around a small dining table, as singers belted out their songs on TV, and our chopsticks made sharp sounds on the white porcelain plates. But now I was lying under my blankets, feeling as if I were in an ice cave.

Zou Zou, I don't want to continue the journey. It will never be free of bumps and it leads into darkness. All the street lamps have been knocked out by people who preceded me on that path. Sometimes the path rises under your feet, leading you to believe you can walk straight to heaven, but the next moment it dips precipitously. Don't give up yet. I know you just needed some rest. This is not the first time. Zou Zou tucked my blankets in. Where's my boyfriend? He went to the drugstore to get some medicine for you. She pointed with her right arm. What she pointed at was a wall, a wall 28 stories high. I knew. He had left me, he too. I muttered to myself sadly. But I am by your side, Zou Zou said slowly and clearly, laying her hand on my forehead, a cool touch that had softness to it. The lumps of dough shrank a little. Tell me where he is? I told you he went to get medicine for you, Zou Zou raised her voice resentfully. Look at what has become of you! She held a mirror up to me and I saw my face with a wooden expression and lifeless eyes. I only need some rest. When I am well again I will continue the journey. This fever is nothing, just don't let it cook your brain, Zou Zou cautioned. Let's wait for his return. Everything will be okay and the darkness will be behind us, Zou Zou began to wax lyrical. She lifted her head, hoping to see the sky, but instead saw only the ceiling. Light appears so bright because of the contrast with darkness. And the pendulum always swings back, I added.

As we stayed quietly in the room, light started to

gild the edges of the window and the minute hand of the clock ticked.

5

Frankly speaking, I was exhausted lying around in bed all day. I lay quietly by myself most of the time. I only slightly moved my arms or my knees every few hours because of my aching bones. My boyfriend moved about quietly in other rooms, dropping in occasionally to comfort me. He said I suffered from workaholism, though not too seriously. It was a case of excessive stress and nervousness. He also said I was too passionate about writing. Only people living in hardship and suffering will be motivated to pick up the pen, and the pen only aggravates the pain and suffering. It's like a snake swallowing up its own tail. Let's get married, I proposed, I want to live an absolutely ordinary, uneventful life. Wait until you get well. Look at your face! It's still so pale. And so is yours. Why have you let your beard grow so long? Sometimes it was Zou Zou who came in to see me. As her observant eyes swept across my face, I pushed the lumps of dough forward so that their ungainly silhouettes would shield the brilliance of all my wit and intelligence, so that all she saw was an inert body. The literary genius was in hibernation, to the despair of all.

Thus I fell asleep, and woke up. When I found it was my boyfriend sitting by my bed, I would smile to him with my eyes. He would repeat the usual routine: feed me delicious food, say good girl get plenty of rest and sleep, and show me funny little ads. In one such ad, a hollow appeared (women would think they knew what that suggested), a finger stirred, went in and out of there. When the lens zoomed out, it was only a man scratching his armpit. But I kept a wary eye on Zou Zou. She was an inscrutable presence. Sometimes she was quiet, reading a novel in a whisper. At other times, she would suddenly throw herself on me and forced my eyelids open to peek at my thoughts. Fortunately, I was in a drowsy state just before falling asleep. Any thoughts that had been there had dispersed in all directions.

In order to solidify the happy life I had been enjoying, my boyfriend and I decided to travel to Wuyuan.

We rented a *siheyuan*-style courtyard house from a farmer. It had a small yard planted with many flowers.

The air was fresh and a quiet settled on the village shortly after dusk. People walked at a leisurely gait, and the sound of motorcycles was like the sizzling made by water mixed with hot oil, dying out after a few pops. My boyfriend chose a romantic white for window curtains, with a frilly bottom edge. I bought us two pairs of goatskin slippers smelling of new leather. We wore the slippers as we walked around in the yard or when we lounged in the sun. I often told my boyfriend how I loved sunshine. For some reason some childhood scenes suddenly came to my mind. For a period I was enamored of erasers of different colors. There was a kind of fragrant erasers that came in pleasant fruit colors. There were even erasers transparent like fruit jellies. I took great care in preserving the transparent wrapping. I also liked letter paper. Sheets printed with pictures were more expensive than colored ones. On the eve of the birthdays of my good friends, I would write, with a fountain pen, on sheets of letter paper, long letters to them. Then I would fold them into origami crane shapes to be put in their pencil cases the following day. They also wrote similar letters to me, but they preferred ballpoint pens. I wrote my first love letter at sixteen. I also wrote letters to my mother and my teachers. I understand now. Those letters were your warm-up exercises. As a result of writing those letters you became a writer, my boyfriend said, looking at me with a faint smile on his face. You have your birthday in a month and a half. I'll write a letter to you too and will tell you a lot of things in it. I only hope you get well and we can do so many things together. You will be lovely that way. We will live on my parents' farm with horses and cows, surrounded by fields and, beyond them, is the sea. The flowers here are not fragrant, I said, drawing myself up from sniffing them. We can plant herbs on the farm. They give off a strong scent. You can imagine that kind of rustic life, where every room is spacious and bright, with snow white starched bed sheets. We can have a big dog. Very idyllic, I agreed.

We could talk forever about my childhood and his farm, never lacking for topics. I loved revisiting those periods time and again, preferably the pre-school years, before my mother gave me the dictionary of idiomatic expressions to memorize. My life after that was a long corridor of time lost in my dealings with words. Even now, whenever I thought of the look on my mother's face when she showed my first composition to relatives and friends, I would give my head a quick shake so that the smug look on her face would be ejected from my head and fly over the fence. In that quiet and happy stretch of memory lasting from age one to five, there was a shelduck weighing three pounds. It waddled about in the house as if it was the master. My mother tied a red ribbon on its neck and named it Duck Lily. It laid an egg every day. My mother started feeding it before the start of the Chinese New Year. When the May came around, the neighborhood committee's women would come to our door and tell us keeping live poultry was forbidden in the city. Actually I was adopted by my mother long after the duck died, but by dint of my mother's repeating the story countless times, it became part of my memory.

My future mother-in-law sent an invitation to me and told me in a separate letter that there was no need for further delay, that we should make up our mind once and for all to marry or to break up. Love takes first place in life, she wrote. But the formalities involved in foreign travel could not be completed overnight. She also told me she was surprised to know I had given up my writing career, saying she had told her friends her son's other half was a writer. Writing takes up too much of my time, and I wish now to have my life back, I explained in my letter of reply. I thought of sending a few Prix Femina books to you, but now I am sending you this very special booklet about herbal cooking instead, my future mother-in-law wrote on the first page of that colorful booklet.

I downloaded and printed the requisite forms from the web and filled in the blanks with reverence and a smile on my face. I made sure every letter leaned at a sixty degree angle (my mother trained me in the art of writing English alphabet letters in cursive. She bought a Hero-brand fountain pen expressly for this purpose. The pen flowed across the paper with incomparable ease and smoothness). My boyfriend accompanied me on my shopping sorties, waiting to see me try on the coats, the boots and the short wool skirts. Choosing presents for members of his family proved great fun. I examined the traditional Chinese paintings reproduced by the watercolor block printing technique and explained to him the difference between Huang Binhong and Huang Feihong. In a pleasant online chat between me and my future father-in-law, he suggested I get a job as a museum guide. Of course, I don't mean immediately. You have to appreciate the beauty of France first before you could think about how to organize your life. In that chat lasting about fifteen minutes, he told me that life in France was very expensive. Yes, yes! I nodded at the webcam, my thought inevitably drawn to the book fees my mother was keeping for me. The sum was not large enough and might not help us afford a decent life, even for three months. Therefore, you may need to find some side jobs, my future father-in-law continued, and it's hard to find a job in France. I held my breath in anticipation of another twist in his conversation. We are ready. In the beginning, we suppose you can live with us if you like, until ... Good! Welcome to France! We will be your guides.

People around me begin to envy, in a way I find quite pleasant, the life I am living now. My girlfriend gave me a set of "Chansons of France" CDs, believing that my voice would become as soft and velvety as the female voice on those CDs. Another girlfriend of mine gave me a set of French-brand bras that had cups the size of my palm but a silky feel. My mother suddenly realized she was losing me, and phoned me with increasing frequency. She asked in addition that I spend one evening with her every week. At the dining table she tried all kinds of tricks to find out details about my sex life. She even asked in a naïve tone: are they really very big between their legs?

But there are always times when I inevitably was by myself. Once I spotted Zou Zou in unfiltered sunlight. She sat with her back to me, her forehead supported on her hands. I thought she was thinking about something. She seemed to have shrunk and wilted a lot. I didn't want to see what her face looked like now, but she turned her head toward me. Don't abandon me, her eyes were opened wide and a tear that had quivered in her eye for a long while and finally fell down her cheek. My father and my mother abandoned me when I was three. They cursed the heavens for not granting them a son. A death certificate was issued for the poor little girl for the price of a meal. She was left in the streets of Shanghai, have you forgotten that? She stood at the side of the street, with a plaque hanging on her chest bearing her birth date. She hung her head and twisted her hands in fear. A crowd began to gather around her, not knowing that the little girl standing before them, being gawked at by them, would one day become a famous writer. I lowered my gaze, avoiding the sight of her face faintly flushed because of her agitation, and shifted my attention to the ground, on which lay some crumbs of broken crackers being attacked by an army of ants. As a child I loved to study, for long hours, the trails of the ants. There is a greater happiness, but you are uninterested, she shouted, all the while coming closer to me. I got scared and rose from the chair in a panic and found myself lying on the floor. My boyfriend called from the kitchen: the soup is ready! So, it was a dream.

I picked myself up half-heartedly. In the dining room the candles had been lit, emitting a dim light. The smell of vegetable soup floated in the air. My boyfriend, with his eyes flashing, was waiting for me with the soup ladle raised. He didn't know that beyond all this there was a shrinking and wilting Zou Zou. I could sense her shivering beside me, as if she could fall into my lap any minute. I lowered my gaze a few times to look carefully at my lap. Once, I could feel her hand quickly touch mine. Yum, it tastes great, I looked at my boyfriend adoringly, his brown curly hair, and the expression on his face as he laughed with his mouth wide open at the comic antics on the French TV channel Canal+. I wanted to tell him I felt happy, I really wanted to live the rest of my life like this. But I merely kept on drinking my soup, the pungency of the pepper tickling my throat like the flickering flame of a candle.

Stories by Contemporary Writers from Shanghai

The Little Restaurant
Wang Anyi

A Pair of Jade Frogs
Ye Xin

Forty Roses
Sun Yong

Goodby, Xu Hu!
Zhao Changtian

Vicissitudes of Life
Wang Xiaoying

The Elephant
Chen Cun

Folk Song
Li Xiao

The Messenger's Letter
Sun Ganlu

Ah, Blue Bird
Lu Xing'er

His One and Only
Wang Xiaoyu

When a Baby Is Born
Cheng Naishan

Dissipation
Tang Ying

Paradise on Earth
Zhu Lin

The Most Beautiful Face in the World
Xue Shu

Beautiful Days
Teng Xiaolan

Between Confidantes
Chen Danyan

She She
Zou Zou